"I'm goir

She straig

"Yes, I will. At least until we find out who was asking about you yesterday."

"Jake, you cannot stay at my house. What will people think?"

"Since when do you care what people think?" The woman he'd known before had made a point of flaunting public opinion.

"Since I moved to a small town where everyone knows me. I'm a schoolteacher, for God's sake. I have a reputation to protect."

"So you're telling me nobody here sleeps with anybody else unless they're lawfully married?"

"I'm sure they do, but they're discreet about it."

"So we'll be discreet. Besides, I never said I was going to sleep with you—unless that's what you want...."

ROCKY MOUNTAIN REVENGE

—

CINDI MYERS

HARLEQUIN® INTRIGUE®

Recycling programs
for this product may
not exist in your area.

ISBN-13: 978-0-373-69742-7

ROCKY MOUNTAIN REVENGE

Copyright © 2014 by Cynthia Myers

Printed in U.S.A.

ABOUT THE AUTHOR

Cindi Myers is the author of more than fifty novels. When she's not crafting new romance plots, she enjoys skiing, gardening, cooking, crafting and daydreaming. A lover of small-town life, she lives with her husband and two spoiled dogs in the Colorado mountains.

Books by Cindi Myers

HARLEQUIN INTRIGUE
1475—ROCKY MOUNTAIN REVENGE

HARLEQUIN SUPERROMANCE
1498—A SOLDIER COMES HOME
1530—A MAN TO RELY ON
1548—CHILD'S PLAY
1612—THE FATHER FOR HER SON
1643—HER MOUNTAIN MAN
1667—DANCE WITH THE DOCTOR

HARLEQUIN AMERICAN ROMANCE
1182—MARRIAGE ON HER MIND
1199—THE RIGHT MR. WRONG
1259—THE MAN MOST LIKELY
1268—THE DADDY AUDITION
1287—HER CHRISTMAS WISH

CAST OF CHARACTERS

Anne Gardener—As Elizabeth Giardino, only daughter of a mob boss, she lived the life of a pampered socialite. But when she agreed to testify against her father, Elizabeth had to die, and was reborn as Anne, a small-town schoolteacher in the Witness Security Program. Now Anne is running for her life from killers and isn't sure who she can trust.

Jake Westmoreland—A forensic accountant for the FBI, Jake went undercover to infiltrate the Giardino mob family. He hadn't counted on falling for the mob boss's daughter, or almost losing his life in a mob hit. Now he's out for revenge on Sam Giardino and his family.

Sam Giardino—The powerful head of the Giardino crime family will stop at nothing to silence those who jeopardize his freedom, including his daughter and her former lover.

Sammy Giardino—Sam's son is next in line to head the crime family, but in the meantime he gets no respect from his father and has no power. Helping the authorities find his father could be his ticket to the control he craves.

Patrick Thompson—The U.S. marshal is sworn to protect Anne from her father and from anyone else who might harm her. He's skeptical of Jake, who he sees as a rogue agent and someone who is possibly unstable.

Chapter One

Elizabeth Giardino had died on February 14. For three hundred and sixty-four days, Anne Gardener had avoided thinking about that terrible day, but on the anniversary of Elizabeth's death, she allowed herself a few minutes of mourning. She stood in her classroom at the end of the day, surrounded by the hearts-and-lace decorations her students had made, and let the memories wash over her: Elizabeth, never Betsy or Beth, her hair streaked with brilliant purple, leaning dangerously far over the balcony of her father's penthouse in Manhattan, waving to the paparazzi who clicked off shot after shot from the apartment below. Elizabeth, in a ten-thousand-dollar designer gown and impossibly high heels, sipping five-hundred-dollar champagne and dancing into the wee hours at a St. Tropez nightclub while a trio of morose men in black suits looked on. Elizabeth, blood staining the breast of her white dress, screaming as those same men dragged her away.

Anne closed her eyes, shutting out the last image. She'd gain nothing by remembering those moments. The past was the past and couldn't be undone.

Yet she couldn't shake a feeling of uneasiness. She looked out the window, at the picture-postcard view of snow-capped mountains against a turquoise sky. Rogers, Colorado, might have been on another planet, for all it resembled New York City. Those lofty peaks did have a mesmerizing effect, anchoring you to the earth in a way. Part of her would like to stay here forever, too, but she doubted she would. In a year, or two at most, she'd have to move on. She couldn't afford to put down roots.

She drew a deep breath, collecting herself, then gathered up her purse and tote bag, and shrugged into her coat. She locked the door of her classroom and walked to the parking lot, her low-heeled boots clicking on the scuffed linoleum, echoing in the empty hallway.

Her parking space was close to the side entrance, directly under a security light that glowed most mornings when she arrived. But there was no need for the light today, though the shadows were beginning to lengthen as the February sun slid down toward its nightly hiding place behind the mountains.

The sudden descent to darkness had made her uneasy when she'd first arrived here. Now she accepted it as part of the environment, along with stunning bright sun that shone despite bitter cold, or the sudden snowstorms that buried the town in two feet of whiteness as soft and dry as powdered sugar.

She drove carefully through town, checking her rearview mirror often. People waved and she returned their greetings. That, too, had unsettled her at first, how people she'd never met greeted her as an old friend within a few days of her arrival. She'd never lived in a small town before, and had to get used to the idea that of course everyone knew the new elementary schoolteacher.

Dealing with the men had been the biggest challenge

at first. More men than women lived in these mountains, she'd been told, and the arrival of an attractive young woman who was clearly unattached drew them like elk to a salt lick. Elizabeth would have been in heaven— the men were ski instructors, mountain climbers, cowboys, miners—all young and fit, rugged and handsome, straight out of a beer commercial or a romance novel. But Anne rebuffed them all, as politely as she could. She wasn't interested in dating anyone. Period.

A rumor had started that her heart had been broken in New York and this was why she'd come west. The sympathetic looks directed her way after this story circulated were almost worse than the men's relentless pursuit.

Things had calmed down after a few months. People had accepted that the new teacher was "standoffish," but that didn't stop them from being friendly and kind and concerned, though she suspected some of this was merely a front for their nosiness. People wanted to know her story and she had none to tell them.

She stopped at the only grocery in town to buy a frozen dinner and the makings of a salad, then drove the back way home. She tried to vary her route every few days, which wasn't easy. There were only so many ways to reach the small house in a quiet subdivision three miles from town.

The house, painted pale green with buff trim, sat in the middle of the block. It had a one-car garage and a sharply peaked roof, and a covered front porch barely large enough for a single Adirondack chair, which still wore a dusting of snow from the last storm.

She unlocked the door and stood for a moment surveying the room. A sofa and chair, covered with a faded

floral print, filled most of the small living room, the
television balanced on an old-fashioned mahogany table
with barley-twist legs. An oval wooden coffee table
and a brass lamp completed the room's furnishings,
aside from a landscape print on the side wall. The place
had come furnished. None of the items were things she
would have picked out, but she'd grown accustomed
to them. No sense changing things around when she
couldn't stay.

She stooped and picked up her mail from the floor,
where it had fallen when the carrier had shoved it
through the slot. Utility bills, the local paper, junk—the
usual. Nothing was amiss about the mail or the house,
yet she couldn't shake her uneasiness. She eased out of
the boots and padded into the kitchen in stocking feet
and put away the groceries. She wished she had a drink.
She had no liquor in the house—she hadn't had a drink
since she'd left New York. It seemed safer that way, to
always be alert. But today she'd welcome the dulling of
her senses, the softening of the sharp edges of feeling.

She put water on for tea instead, then went into the
bedroom to change into jeans and a comfy sweater.
Maybe she'd start a fire in the small woodstove in the
living room, and try to lose herself in a novel.

The bedroom held the only piece of furniture in the
house she really liked—an antique cherry sleigh bed,
the wood burnished by years of use to a soft patina. She
trailed one hand across the satin finish on her way to
the closet. She stopped beside the only other piece of
furniture in the room, a sagging armchair, and slipped
out of the corduroy skirt and cotton turtleneck. Sensible
clothes for racing after six-year-olds. Elizabeth would
have laughed to see her in them.

She opened the closet and reached for a pair of jeans. She scarcely had time to register the presence of another person in the room when strong arms wrapped around her in a grip like iron. A hand clamped over her mouth, stifling her scream. Panic swept over her, blinding her. She fought with everything she had against this unknown assailant, but he held her fast.

"Shhh, shhh. It's all right. I won't hurt you." The man's voice was soft in her ear, its gentleness at odds with the strength that bound her. "Look at me."

He loosened his hold enough that she could turn her head to look at him. She screamed again as recognition shook her and choked on the sound as she stared into the eyes of a dead man.

Jake Westmoreland watched the woman in his arms closely, trying to judge if it was safe to uncover her mouth. He wasn't ready to release his hold on her yet. Not because he feared she'd strike out at him, but because he'd waited so many months to hold her again.

She was thinner than he remembered, fragile as a bird in his hands, where he'd never thought of her as fragile before. Her hair was darker too, cut differently, and the bright streaks of color were gone. He'd seen her picture, so he should have been prepared for that. But nothing could have really prepared him for meeting her again, not after the trauma of their last parting. For months, he hadn't even been sure she was still alive.

"I thought you were dead," she said when he did remove his hand from her mouth. Tears brimmed in her eyes, glittering on her lashes.

"I was sure Giardino's goons would go after you next."

"Your friends got to me first. But they never told me

you were still alive. How? The last time I saw you…" She shook her head. "So much blood…"

They told him later he had died, there on the floor of the suite at the Waldorf Astoria. But the trauma team had shocked his heart back to life and poured liters of blood into him to keep his organs from shutting down. He'd spent weeks in the hospital and months after that in rehab—months lying in bed with nothing to do but think about her.

He brushed her hair back from her temples, as if to reassure himself she was real, and not a dream. "Elizabeth, I—"

The pain in her eyes pierced him. "It's Anne. Elizabeth doesn't exist anymore. She died that day at the hotel."

He'd known this, too, but in the moment his emotions had gotten the better of him. He stepped back, releasing her at last. "Why Anne?"

"It was my middle name." Her bottom lip curved slightly in the beginnings of the teasing smile he'd come to know so well. The old smile he'd missed so much. "You didn't know?"

"No." There was so much he hadn't known about her. "Can we sit down and talk?" He nodded toward the bed, the only place where two people could sit in the room.

A piercing whistle rent the air. He had his gun out of his shoulder holster before he even had time to think.

She stared at the weapon with an expression of disgust. "Are you going to shoot my tea kettle?"

He put the gun away.

"Let's go into the living room," she said. She pulled a robe from a hook on the closet door and wrapped it around herself, but not before he took in the full breasts rounded at the top of her black lace bra, the narrow waist fanning out to slim hips—and the scar on her lower back.

"Your tattoo's gone," he said. She'd had the words *Nil opus captivis* at the base of her spine, in delicate script. *Take no prisoners*. The motto of a woman who'd been determined to wring everything she could from life.

"I had it removed. They told me I shouldn't leave any identifying marks."

She led the way into the living room, going first to the kitchen to turn off the burner beneath the kettle, then to the front window to pull the blinds closed. He sat on the sofa, expecting she would sit beside him, but she retreated to the chair, her arms wrapped protectively around her middle.

"How did you find me?" she asked.

"I still have friends at the Bureau. People who owe me favors."

"No one is supposed to know where I am. They promised—" She broke off, her lips pressed together in a thin line. He could read the rest of her thoughts in her eyes. This wasn't the first time the government had broken promises to her. What about all the promises *he'd* made?

"I never meant to lie to you," he said. "I was trying to protect you."

"You didn't do a very good job of that, did you?"

He clenched his hands into fists. "No. Tell me what happened after I left. I heard you turned state's evidence."

"If you're still with the FBI you should know all this."

"I'm not with the Bureau anymore."

She raised her brows. "Oh? Why not?"

"Officially, I was retired on disability."

"And unofficially?"

"Unofficially, they thought I was too much of a risk."

"Because of what happened with my father?"

"That, and…other things." He'd committed the cardinal sin of developing an intimate relationship with a person he was supposed to be investigating. Not that Elizabeth Giardino had been the target of his investigations, but she was close enough to her father to raise questions about Jake's integrity and his ability to perform his job. "Tell me what happened after I was shot," he said.

"My father's goons did try to drag me away, but they didn't know you had the place surrounded. When the cops broke in, everyone was too focused on keeping my father safe to worry about me. Someone hustled me into a car and took me downtown."

He tried to imagine the scene. She'd been covered in his blood, wild with fear. They'd have put her in an interrogation room and turned up the pressure, grilling her for hours, trying to break her. At one time he would have said she wasn't a woman who could be broken, but now he wasn't so sure. "They wanted you to provide evidence against your father."

"They didn't have to persuade me. After I saw what he did to you…I wanted to make him pay."

Was it because of him, really? Or because her father had destroyed her trust? In one blast of gunfire she'd gone from pampered daddy's girl to enemy number one. It must have made her question everything.

"I laid all the family's dirty secrets out in public and he swore he'd kill me," she continued. "He stood there in court and cursed me and said I was dead to him already." She swallowed, and he sensed the effort it took for her to rein in her emotions.

"After that it was too dangerous for you to remain in New York," he said.

She nodded. "It was too dangerous for me to be me. Within a month my father had escaped prison and disappeared, but we all know he's still out there somewhere, and he hasn't forgotten anything. The feds gave me a new identity. Elizabeth Giardino died in a tragic boating accident in the Caribbean and Anne Gardener came to Rogers, Colorado, to teach school."

"I never imagined you as a schoolteacher."

"I had a degree in English from Barnard. The Marshals Service pulled a few strings to get me my teaching certificate. They found this job for me, and this house." She looked around the room. The plain, old-fashioned furniture was as unlike her hip Manhattan apartment as he could have imagined. "I suppose they thought this place was as anonymous as a town could be." Her gaze shifted back to him. "Yet you found me."

"I had inside information."

"Other people can pay for information."

Other people being her father and his goons. "I knew about this place. That it was on a list of possible hideouts. I persuaded a former colleague to let me take a look at the accounting records for the period after you disappeared and I found payment to a Colorado bank. I was able to trace that to this house."

"But you still didn't know I was here."

"I looked online, through the archives of the local paper. I saw the announcement last summer about the new teacher. The timing was right, and I thought it might be you."

"You make it sound easy."

"Not so easy. There are a lot of layers between you and the feds. Layers I helped design."

"I forgot you started out as an accountant." She gave a rueful laugh. "Not the picture most people have of the rough-and-tough federal agent."

He'd been hired straight out of university to work as a forensic accountant for the Bureau. Following the money put away more criminals than shootouts. But then they'd needed someone to go undercover in the Giardino family and he'd volunteered, wanting a change from sitting behind a desk. He hadn't counted on getting in so deep. He hadn't counted on Elizabeth.

"How are you doing?" he asked. "Do you like it here?"

"I don't dislike it. The people are friendly. I love the children."

He tried to imagine her surrounded by first graders. He'd never thought of her as the mothering type, yet the image seemed to suit this new, quieter side of her. "It's very different from the life you lived before," he said.

"I'm very different."

"Yeah." A person didn't go through the kinds of things they'd been through without some change. "How are you doing, really?" he asked.

"How do you think?" Her voice was hard, the accusation in her eyes like acid poured on his wounds. "It's hard. And exhausting, being afraid all the time."

"You don't feel safe?"

"You of all people should know the answer to that. You know my father—he'll do anything to get his way.

And he meant it when he said he would see that I was dead. If you found me, he can too. Why did you come here?"

"I wanted to see you."

"Well, you've seen me. Now you can leave." She stood, and cinched the robe tighter around her waist.

He rose also. "Eli—Anne. Listen to me. I need your help."

"For what?"

"I need you to help me find your father."

"Why? You said you're no longer with the Bureau."

"No. But if we find him he'll go back to prison—and they won't let him escape this time."

"I can't help you. All I want is to stay as far away from him as possible."

"Don't you want to put an end to this? Don't you want to be safe again?"

"What are you talking about?"

"I'm talking about finding your father and making sure he's punished the way he deserves."

"Revenge?" She spat the word, like a curse. "You want revenge?"

"Call it that if you want. Or call it justice. He's killed too many people. Someone has to stop him."

"Well, that someone won't be me."

"I'm not asking you to risk anything. I just want you to talk to me. To tell me where he might be hiding."

"I already gave you everything I could. Why do you want more?"

She had given him everything—her body and her beauty and a willingness to risk that had made his own bravery seem a sham in comparison. "I need your help," he said again.

"You're as bad as he is—you only want to use people to get what you want." Without another glance at
him she left the room, the door to the bedroom clicking softly shut behind her.

He stared after her, feeling sick. Maybe her words
hurt so much because they were too close to the truth.
He did want to use her. She was the only link he had
to Sam Giardino. The only way he could do what he
had to do.

Chapter Two

Anne leaned against the closed bedroom door, her ear pressed to the wood, listening. The silence in the house was so absolute she imagined she could hear Jake's heart beating—though of course it was only the frantic pounding in her own chest. Footsteps crossed the room, moving away from her, the heavy, deliberate echo of each step moving through her like the aftershock of an earthquake. She bit her lip to keep from shouting at him not to leave. Of course she wanted him to leave. She didn't want any part of the kind of danger he represented.

The front door closed with a solid click. She held her breath, and heard the muffled roar of a car engine coming to life. The sound faded and she was alone. She moved away from the door and sagged onto the bed, waiting for the tears that wouldn't come. She'd cried them all out that night at the hotel, believing he was dead, knowing her life had ended.

Jake. One of the other agents at the Bureau had laughed when she'd called him that. "You mean Jacob? No one ever calls him Jake."

No one but her. And everyone in her family. It was the way he'd first introduced himself to them. His name—but not his name. Like everything else about him, he'd built a lie around a kernel of truth. He wasn't really a low-level official with the Port Authority, wanting to get in on the Giardino family business. He was an undercover operative for the FBI. Not even a real cop, but an accountant.

By the time she'd learned all this it had been too late. She had already been in love with him.

So what was he doing back in her life now? Hadn't he done enough to ruin her? Before he came along she'd been happy. She'd had everything—looks, money, friends, family. She wasn't an idiot—she'd known her father didn't always operate on the right side of the law. He'd probably done some very bad things. But those things didn't concern her. They didn't touch the perfect life she'd built for herself.

Jake had made her take off the blinders and see the painful truth about who her father was.

About who she really was.

She pushed herself off the bed, pushing away the old fear and despair with the movement. Not letting herself stop to think, she dressed, grabbed her keys and headed out the door. She couldn't sit in this house one more minute or she'd go crazy.

She drove back into town, to the little gym one block off Main. A few people looked up from the free weights and treadmills as she passed. She nodded in greeting but didn't stop to talk. She changed into her workout gear, found her gloves and headed for the heavy bag and began throwing jabs and uppercuts, bouncing on her toes the way the gym's owner, a former boxer named McGarrity, had shown her.

She'd taken up boxing when, shortly after her arrival

in Rogers, she'd come to the gym for what was billed as a ladies' self-defense class. Turned out McGarrity's idea of self-defense was teaching women to box. Anne had fallen in love with the sport the first time she landed a solid punch. She'd never been in a position where she had to fight back before. Now, at least, she was prepared to do so.

She'd worked up a sweat and was breathing hard when a woman's voice called her name across the room.

Maggie O'Neal taught second grade in the classroom across the hall from Anne. A curvy woman with brown, curly hair, dressed now in pink yoga pants and a matching hoodie, she was the closest thing Anne had to a best friend. "Maybe I should take up boxing," Maggie said. "You look so healthy and…dewy."

Anne laughed. "I'm sweating like a pig, you mean."

"It looks good on you."

"What are you doing here?"

"I just got out of a yoga class. Marcie Evanston teaches one every afternoon at this time. You should join us sometime."

Anne had tried yoga once. While everyone else lay still in *savasana,* her mind had raced, unable to grow quiet. She needed physical activity—punching the heavy bag or an opponent in the ring—to shut off the voices in her head and drown out the fear.

"Can I talk you into a break for a smoothie or some juice?" Maggie asked.

"Sure."

Anne stashed her gloves in the cubby marked with her name and the two women made their way to the juice bar next door to the gym—McGarrity's latest effort to squeeze more profit out of the facility. The idea seemed to be working—the juice bar was usually busy, favored by tourists and local office people as well as gym members.

They sat at the counter and ordered banana-berry smoothies.

"Look what Ty gave me for Valentine's." Maggie extended her pinky, showing a gold ring with a row of tiny diamonds.

"It's beautiful," Anne said. "Was it a surprise?"

Maggie nodded. "We saw it in the window of a store over in Grand Junction last month and I remarked how I've always wanted a pinkie ring. When I saw the ring box on my plate this morning, I squealed loud enough to wake the next door neighbors." She smiled at the ring. "Did I get lucky or what?"

"You got very lucky." Anne ignored the pinching pain at her heart. In her party-girl days she'd dismissed love as some fanciful notion from novels and movies. She'd liked being with men, but she hadn't needed one to make her happy. And the thought of wanting to spend the rest of her life with one had seemed ludicrous.

And then Jacob Westmoreland—she'd known him as Jake West—had walked up to her at one of her father's clubs and asked her to dance. She'd thought he was handsome and a decent dancer, but then she'd looked into his eyes and her world had shifted. A flood of lust and longing and locked-in connection had rocked her like a tidal wave. Nothing had ever been the same after that.

And now he was back. She didn't have the strength to go through that heartache again.

"Did you see your picture in the paper? Great promo for the carnival."

Anne realized Maggie had been talking for several minutes about something. "My picture?"

"In the Telluride paper today. You made the front page."

She fought back the nervous flutter in her stomach. "I don't remember anyone taking my picture."

"You remember that reporter who came around Saturday, when we were working on our carnival booth? He must have taken some candid shots after he talked to us. He got a perfect picture of you framed by the heart cutout in the side of the booth. I think you leaned out to say something to Ty."

"He should have asked me before publishing it."

"Oh, come on! I know you don't like having your picture taken, but it was a great shot, I promise. I'll save my copy for you. And maybe it will pull in a few more people to our booth at the carnival."

"That's great." Anne managed a weak smile. The first and second grades were teaming up to sell hot chocolate and cider at the Winter Carnival in the town park next weekend, an annual fundraiser for local charities. She wanted to do her part to help, but the thought of her picture circulating in the public made her uneasy. What if someone from her old life saw?

She shrugged off the thought. After all, it was just a small-town paper, a very long way from New York.

"Hey, ladies, how you doing?" A stocky man with broad shoulders and a shaved head came to stand beside their bar stools. Evan McGarrity was rumored to be in his sixties, but he looked two decades younger, and had the energy of a man half his age. "Annie, did your friend find you?" he asked.

Anne went cold. "What friend?"

"There was a guy in here earlier, asking about you. Said he was a friend of yours from New York."

Aware of Maggie's eyes on her, Anne kept her expression noncommittal. McGarrity must mean Jake. "What did he look like?"

"Not too tall. About my height, maybe. Good set of shoulders on him. Looked like he might have played football. Dark hair. Expensive suit."

Jake was tall, with sandy hair and a slim build. This wasn't Jake. She stood, knocking the half-empty smoothie glass onto its side as she groped blindly for her purse.

"Anne, are you all right?" Maggie asked. "You've gone all gray."

"I'm sorry about the mess." She stared numbly at the purple liquid spreading across the countertop. "I really have to go."

She ran to her car, still dressed in her workout clothes, not feeling the icy evening breeze against her bare legs, ignoring the shouts of her friends behind her.

Someone had found her—someone who wasn't Jake. Someone who might mean her harm.

ANNE'S FIRST INSTINCT was to go to Jake for help. But she had no idea where he was staying. And maybe he'd led them here. She could call Patrick Thompson, the marshal who'd been assigned to her, but he was hours away in Denver. By the time he got here, it might be too late.

She drove home and raced into the house, locking the door behind her. In the bedroom, she dragged her suitcase from the top shelf of the closet and began throwing things in it. She'd wait until after dark, then she'd leave. She'd drive as far as she could toward Denver. It was easier to get lost in the city. She'd ditch the car there, maybe buy a new one or take a bus. She couldn't travel out of the country. The feds wouldn't let her get a passport—letting her leave would be too risky, they said.

But she had to leave. The last time she'd seen him, her father had vowed to erase her. That was the word he'd used—*erase*. As if she were a mistake he needed to blot out. She'd never seen such coldness in his eyes before. His daughter was dead to him already—disposing of her body was of no consequence.

Never mind that she still had plenty of use for that body.

A knock on the door made her freeze. She tried to think. Would the man who was looking for her knock and announce himself?

Yes, she decided, he would. He'd want her to open the door. To let him inside where he could dispose of her quietly, without the neighbors seeing. He'd slip away without anyone noticing and tomorrow, when she didn't show up at class, someone would find her. Someone else would discover her true identity, and the newspapers and gossip magazines would print the news in bold headlines. *Mob King Takes Revenge on Daughter Who Betrayed Him* or *Mafia Princess Gets Hers*.

She waited, but no second knock came. No friendly voice called out in concern. She forced herself to breathe, ragged, metallic-tinged breaths that tasted of terror.

When she could stand the tension no more, she tiptoed into the front room and peered out a gap in the blinds. The street in front of her house was empty. Dark. After another half hour of stillness, she decided no one was there. But maybe they were waiting across the street, waiting for her to open the door.

She pulled on her coat and gloves, then took the loaded pistol from her bedside table and slipped it into the pocket of her coat. When she'd asked for the gun the Marshals had dismissed her, saying she had no need to be armed. She was merely an innocent schoolteacher. Patrick Thompson had assured her the U.S. Marshals Service would provide all the protection she needed. She'd argued with him to no avail.

But three days after her arrival here she'd received a package in the mail. The handgun, ammunition and an unsigned note. *I hope you never need this*, the note read. *But just in case...*

One hand on the pistol, she slipped out the back door. The temperature had dropped twenty degrees with the setting sun. The air was brittle with cold, the ground crisp beneath her feet. Staying close to the side of the house, she moved toward the street. She took a step, then waited, listening. She repeated this process all the way down the side of the house, so that twenty minutes passed before she reached the corner. She craned her head around to look toward her front door.

The small porch was empty, the light shining down on the doormat and a rectangle of white that lay on the mat.

Chapter Three

Anne studied the rectangle of white that gleamed on the doormat. It looked like an envelope, and a simple envelope shouldn't be so ominous. But this one was out of place. The mail carrier delivered letters through the slot in the door. Other people who had messages for her telephoned, or contacted her at school. Did this envelope contain an explosive to injure her, or a poison?

Neither of those things were her father's style. He believed in personal retribution—not necessarily from him, but from his goons. His representatives, he called them. She remembered overhearing him on the phone with a contractor he suspected of double-crossing him. His words had been so calm, in sharp contrast to the menace in his voice. "I'm sending a couple of my representatives over to discuss this with you."

When the police found the man, he was floating in the sound, his face gone. Cut off, she'd heard later, while he was still alive.

Shivering with cold and fear, she turned and raced back around the side of the house and through the back door. She ran to the front, opened the door just wide enough to snatch the envelope from the mat, then sat on the sofa, shaking.

She turned the envelope over and read the childish printing. *Miss Gardener* was rendered in uneven printing. Below that, a more adult hand had penned *Happy Valentine's Day*.

Inside the envelope was a crooked heart cut from construction paper, decorated generously with silver glitter and stickers bearing images of cupids and more hearts. The crayoned signature was from one of her students, a wide-eyed little boy who clearly had a bit of a crush on his teacher.

She stared at the words through a blur of tears, hating how the sordidness of her old life had reached out to taint this sweet, innocent gesture. If she ran away, all of that ugliness would follow her, to whatever new town she settled in.

She had friends here in Rogers. A place in the community. She wasn't ready to give that up, not until she absolutely had to.

"ARE YOU STAYING in town long, Mr. Westmoreland?"

The desk clerk at Rogers's only hotel smiled at Jake, all but batting her eyelashes at him. He returned the smile. It never hurt to be friendly with the locals, especially in a place this small. You never knew who might give you the information you needed, or put you in touch with the one contact who could help you break a case. "A few days. I'm not sure, really." He plucked a brochure advertising Telluride ski area from a rack on the counter. "This is such a beautiful place, I might stay longer than I planned."

"We've got plenty of scenery, that's for sure," she said. "Not much excitement, though."

"I don't need excitement." He'd had enough to last

a lifetime. As soon as he was done with this last job, he'd stick to crunching numbers for the rest of his life.

"You might stick around for the Winter Carnival next weekend," the clerk said. "That's kind of fun."

"What's the Winter Carnival?"

"It's this little festival in City Park. Ice skating, ice sculpture, a broomball tournament. A bonfire. Different groups have booths selling food and hot chocolate and stuff. Real small-town, but a lot of tourists like it."

"I might have to check it out. Thanks." The phone rang, and when she turned away to answer it, he took the opportunity to set the brochure aside and leave before she questioned him further.

Outside, the sun was so bright he squinted even behind his sunglasses. The windshield of the car he'd rented in Grand Junction was thick with frost. He turned the heat on full blast and sat in the driver's seat, debating his next move.

He'd driven by Anne's house last night, after midnight. Her car had been parked in the driveway, a single light in the back of the house glowing yellow behind the shades. Her bedroom. He'd thought of stopping, but she'd made it clear she wanted nothing to do with him.

Not that he intended to take no for an answer. He understood she was angry with him—upset and hurt by the lies he'd told her. Sooner or later she'd see he'd had to lie to protect them both. The fact that he'd failed so miserably made him more determined than ever to make it up to her.

She was afraid; that was clear. Who wouldn't be, in her position? Helping him would force her to admit that fear—that weakness. For all the changes in her life and her appearance, she was still a woman who never liked to admit any weakness. *Take no prisoners.* She could erase the words from her skin, but Jake was certain they were still inscribed on her heart.

Approaching her at her house had been a tactical error. He could see that now. They needed neutral territory. With other people around she wouldn't be so guarded.

He spent the morning at the library, reading through back issues of the *Rogers Reporter,* learning what Anne's life had been like these past nine months. Other than the announcement of her hiring, the new first-grade teacher had stayed out of the spotlight. She was playing by the rules of the Witness Security Program, keeping quiet and fitting in.

At three o'clock he drove to the school, a low-slung group of buildings set one behind the other at the foot of a mesa. The elementary classrooms were in the last building, next to a fenced playground where children in parkas and snowsuits climbed a jungle gym and kicked a soccer ball in the snow.

Jake spotted Anne standing with a shorter woman with curly hair. He waved and strode toward them. Anne stiffened, and the other woman eyed him warily, but he kept a pleasant expression on his face. *I come in peace.*

Up close, she looked tired, gray smudges under her eyes, her skin pale beneath the makeup, as if she hadn't slept well. Had thoughts of him kept her awake? Memories of what had happened between them? "Hello, Anne," he said, stopping in front of her.

"What are you doing here?" She didn't look angry— more resigned, he decided.

"I was hoping I could take you for a cup of coffee."

He was aware of the other woman staring at him, suspicion in her eyes.

"Is this the man McGarrity was talking about?" the woman asked.

"What man?" Jake asked. "Who's McGarrity?"

Anne shook her head. "This isn't him."

Jake turned to the other woman and offered his hand. "I'm Jake Westmoreland. A friend of Anne's from New York."

"Margaret O'Neal." Her hand brushed his lightly before retreating. "Anne doesn't look like she wants to see you."

"It's been a long time. I wanted to apologize for what happened the last time we met."

"What happened?" Margaret and Jake were the only ones talking, but at least Anne was listening. She hadn't walked away.

"Anne left before I could say goodbye." He spoke to Margaret, but his gaze remained fixed on Anne. She stood with her arms folded, her body angled away from him, her shoulders stiff with tension. "I've always regretted that."

"We don't have anything to say to each other," Anne said.

"We have a lot to say to each other. I came two thousand miles to talk to you. Please don't turn me away now."

"You can't say no to a man who says please." Margaret touched her friend's shoulder. "A cup of coffee can't hurt."

Anne's eyes telegraphed the word "traitor" to her friend, but she kept silent. She glanced at Jake. "One cup of coffee, then you leave me alone."

"One cup of coffee." He wouldn't leave her, though. He couldn't.

"Call me," Margaret said, and left them, smiling to herself.

Anne moved closer to Jake. "Now you've done it," she whispered.

"Done what?"

"Everyone will think you're the long-lost boyfriend who broke my heart."

The words were so melodramatic they were almost comical, but he felt the pain behind them. "Is that what happened, Anne?" he asked, his voice as gentle as he could make it.

"No!" Her eyes sparked with anger, the energy in them a jolt to his system, a glimpse of the woman she'd been. "But it's what people want to think. They think I don't know about the stories they've made up to explain me, but in a town this small, gossip always eventually gets around to everyone. They say I came here all the way from New York to recover from a broken heart. It's the reason I don't date anyone now. The reason I won't talk about my past."

"It's a good story," he said. Maybe part of it was even true, but he didn't say this. He didn't want to risk making her angrier.

"That's the only reason I let them think that. It's a good story."

"Have coffee with me and tell me your real story."

"You already know my real story."

"Then maybe it's time I told you mine."

Her gaze met his, sharp and questioning. "Come with me," he said. "Listen to what I have to say and then decide how you feel."

She hesitated, then nodded. "All right."

She insisted on taking her own car, and led the way to a coffee shop tucked between the library and a church. At this time of day the place was practically deserted, and they settled into a pair of upholstered wing chairs, facing each other across a low table. She cradled her coffee cup in both hands, legs crossed, back straight, elegant even in her schoolteacher's denim skirt and turtleneck sweater. "Tell me your story, Jake," she said. "Or should I call you Jacob?"

"I always liked the way Jake sounded when you said it."

"But Jake West wasn't your real name."

"No. But Jake West was close enough to Jacob Westmoreland my handlers thought I wouldn't get confused in a tense situation." He shifted, balancing his coffee cup on the arm of the chair. "I wasn't even supposed to be there at all. I was auditing the accounts at one of your father's companies, looking for some proof of mob connections. I needed some more information so I made a personal visit. Completely unauthorized, but when I hit it off with the manager there, my bosses saw a way in. They gave me a crash course in undercover work and sent me off to find out what I could. They never expected I'd blow the whole organization open."

She traced one finger down the side of her cup. Her nails were short and unvarnished, different from the perfect manicure she'd always sported before. "Was seducing me part of the plan?"

"You were never part of the plan," he said. "I didn't even know you existed until I saw you at the club that night."

"You were investigating my father and you didn't know about me?" She looked scornful.

"I was investigating his business. I didn't care about his personal life. And I don't read the society pages."

"Why did you dance with me that first night?"

"Because I couldn't not dance with you. The moment I saw you, we might as well have been the only two people in the room." He leaned toward her. "Don't tell me you didn't feel it, too."

She looked down at her lap, avoiding his gaze, but the blush in her cheeks warmed. "Yes," she breathed, scarcely louder than a whisper.

Attraction pulled at him now, as strongly as that first night. He'd arrived at the club late—almost midnight. Andy, the manager he'd befriended, who was one of Sam Giardino's lieutenants, had invited him for drinks. A social call, though Jake suspected this was the night he was going to meet Sam himself.

He and Andy had been standing at the railing overlooking the dance floor of the club in the East Village. A D.J. played techno-pop too loudly and dozens of young people crowded the dance floor. How he'd even spotted her in the confusion was a mystery, but his gaze had zeroed in on her like a laser. She had been dancing with a group of girlfriends, hands in the air, twirling. Laughing with such joy. He'd stared, knowing for the first time what the word "gobsmacked" really meant. He'd never seen someone so full of life and energy. So beautiful and vibrant.

And he'd never wanted anyone so much. Forgetting why he was there and all he might be risking, he'd pushed his way through the crowd until he'd stood in front of her. She'd immediately lowered her arms, and her smile had faded. "Dance with me," he'd said.

"Why should I?" she'd asked, her voice cool.

"Because I asked nicely." He'd smiled, coaxing her. "Please."

He'd expected a few moments' dancing facing each other, not touching even, but she'd surprised him by moving into his arms. As if the deejay played only for her, the music had switched to a slow number. She'd cuddled up to him like a kitten, and laid her head on his shoulder. "If you want to dance with me, you have to do it properly," she'd cooed.

And that was how he'd met Sam Giardino, with the don's daughter wrapped around him, closer than any father likes to see his daughter next to another man. Of course, he hadn't known she was Giardino's daughter, but the horrified look on Andy's face clued him in that something was very wrong. When Elizabeth had stepped back and murmured, "This is my father," he figured he'd just made the biggest mistake of his career.

But Sam had surprised him. "Elizabeth is a very good judge of character," he'd declared. "If she likes you, I like you."

And that was it. With one dance he'd gone from suspicious stranger to practically a member of the family. Weeks went by when he scarcely returned to his own apartment, living at the Giardino penthouse in Manhattan. He ate dinner with the family four nights out of five. He saw Elizabeth every day. And he collected reams of evidence he hoped to use to one day put her father away. His work never felt like a betrayal of her; she was too good for her father. Jake was going to rescue her from that life.

He'd never asked if she wanted rescuing. He could see now that had been a mistake. "I'm sorry things worked out the way they did," he said.

"It could have been worse. At least we're both still alive." She sipped her coffee. "Elizabeth's gone, but I'm still here."

"Are you okay with that?"

"Would I rather be living the life of the carefree, wealthy socialite in the most exciting city in the world?" She shook her head. "Even if it was possible, I couldn't go back to that life—not after you showed me what was really going on, where the money that paid for my designer clothes and nights on the town really came from."

"I always knew there was more to you than most people gave you credit for."

"Right. They didn't give me much credit after my father was arrested. If I wasn't the poor little rich girl who was biting the hand that fed her, I was the gold-plated harpy who was no better than a criminal herself."

"I guess I missed all that."

"How long were you in the hospital?"

"Five weeks. Then I was in a rehab facility for four months after that."

"Why aren't you in the witness protection program?" she asked. "If my father knows you're alive he'll do everything he can to change that."

"You thought I was dead—he probably does, too. And even if he doesn't, I fought too hard to keep my life to turn around and leave it behind. Not that I blame you for making that choice."

"Maybe it was easier for me because I didn't want to be who I was anymore. But I still don't feel safe. Aren't you afraid?"

"If I let myself think about the danger, I'd be afraid. But I've learned to put it out of my mind."

"To compartmentalize."

"Is that what it's called?"

"The marshal who's assigned to me—a guy named Patrick Thompson—used to talk about it. He told me that's what I had to learn to do—to lock the fear away in a separate part of my mind and not let it out, like a file I'd sealed."

"Good advice. Did you take it?"

"I tried. It works sometimes. And then something happens to remind me…." She looked away, her lower lip caught between her teeth.

"Has something happened lately?" he asked. "Something that's made you afraid again?"

She didn't answer, and kept her face turned away from him. He leaned forward and took her chin in his hand, gently turning her head until her eyes met his. "Tell me."

Chapter Four

Jake noticed Anne's hesitation, as if she was debating whether to trust him. "I'm the only one who knows your story," he said softly. "The only one who can understand what you're going through."

She took a long sip of coffee, then set the cup down and looked him in the eye. "Yesterday, after we talked, I went to my gym. The owner told me a man had been in there asking about me. Was that you?"

He shook his head. "I haven't been to any gym. And I didn't ask anyone in Rogers about you. I came straight to your house as soon as I got here."

The lines around her eyes deepened. "McGarrity—that's the gym owner—said this guy was dark, and built like a football player."

"Could be one of your father's goons."

"Yes. It could be." Her shoulders sagged. "I started to leave last night—to throw what I could in the car and just…run away."

"Why didn't you?"

"What would that solve? I'd still be afraid, and alone. More alone even than I am now. I like it here. I've made friends. And there are people here who depend on me. Kids. I don't want to let them down."

"You've always been a fighter. That's one of the things that drew me in. Even that first night on the dance floor, you made your own rules. Everyone else had to follow them or get out of your way."

"You make me sound like a pushy witch."

"You could be that, too. But it's kept you alive."

She shook her head. "I'm not like that anymore. I've learned the wisdom of staying in the background and letting others take the lead. I just want to do my job and live a quiet life."

"Wouldn't it be better if you didn't have to be afraid?"

"You mean if my father weren't around to threaten me?"

"Yes."

"I'm not going to help you, Jake. I did what I could to punish my father and I wasted my breath."

"You won't be wasting your breath this time."

"What are you going to do? You're not with the Bureau anymore. You don't have any authority. If the government can't find Sam Giardino, with all their resources, what makes you think you'll have better luck?"

"You know your father better than anyone. You know his habits and the people he associates with. The places he likes to vacation and where he stays when he goes out of town."

"You can learn all those things without me. Your friends in the Bureau have files filled with that kind of information."

"They know facts. They don't know emotions, or the reasons your father does what he does. You can tell me those things. You can help me predict what he's going to do next."

"And then what? You confront him and end up dead yourself? Or you lead him to me and I'm dead?"

"I won't let anything happen to you. I promise."

"You can't make that promise. Not when so much is out of your control."

"I'm going to stay with you tonight."

She straightened. "You will not."

"Yes, I will. At least until we find out who was asking about you at your gym yesterday."

"Jake, you cannot stay at my house. What will people think?"

"Since when do you care what people think?" The woman he'd known before had made a point of flaunting public opinion.

"Since I moved to a small town where everyone knows me. I'm a schoolteacher, for God's sake. I have a reputation to protect."

"And me spending the night with you is going to ruin that reputation? You're a grown woman."

"This isn't New York. Some people here still care about morality."

"So you're telling me nobody here sleeps with anybody else unless they're lawfully married?"

"I'm sure they do, but they're discreet about it."

"So we'll be discreet. Besides, I never said I was going to sleep with you—unless that's what you want."

The color rose in her cheeks. "It doesn't matter what we're actually doing. It's what they think we're doing."

"But I'm the long-lost boyfriend come back to beg forgiveness," he said. "Doesn't everyone love a lover?"

"No. You can't stay with me."

"Fine. Then you come stay with me. At the hotel."

"That's even worse. Sneaking off to a hotel together."

He laughed. "We're just a sordid pair. Honestly, I think you're making something out of nothing."

"You don't live here. I do. And I don't want to do anything to call attention to myself."

"Too late for that. I'm here. And this other mysterious stranger is here, asking about you. What are people going to say about that? The new teacher's gotten very popular all of a sudden."

"Just go away, Jake. Please? I'll handle this on my own."

"No."

"You don't think I can handle this?"

"I'm not going to leave you. Not until I know you're safe."

"I'll call the Marshals office in Denver. They'll send someone to babysit me for a while."

"Another strange man come to town to hang out with the teacher. Won't that set people talking?"

She made a face. "Maybe they'll send a woman. I'll tell people she's my sister."

"Then tell them I'm your brother."

"As if anyone would believe that."

"Why not? Siblings don't have to look alike."

"You don't act like any brother."

"Maybe not like your brother. What's Sam Junior up to these days?"

"I have no idea. As far as I know, he thinks I'm dead."

"Sammy was what, twenty-four when I saw him last? He'd just had a baby with that woman—what was her name?"

"Stacy. She was the daughter of some guy who owed my father a favor. It was practically an arranged marriage. I don't think she was very happy."

He didn't remember much about the girl, or her husband, for that matter. "Sammy Junior was in law school, wasn't he?"

"Yes. I imagine he has his license by now."

"I guess a lawyer is a handy thing to have in the family when you spend so much time breaking the law."

She stood. "I think it's time for you to go now."

"I'll be over later tonight," he said.

"No!"

"I'll park my car a couple blocks away—near that mechanic, with all the cars in the yard. And I'll leave early, before anyone is up."

"I won't let you in."

She turned away, but he grabbed her wrist and leaned closer, his voice low but insistent. "I can't leave you alone, not with some man neither of us knows asking about you. At least let me protect you until your handler from the Marshals office shows up."

Her eyes told him she hated being in this position—hated having to depend on anyone, but especially him. But she'd always been more intelligent than most people he knew; she could be reckless, but she was never foolish. "All right," she said, and pulled out of his grasp. "But only until the marshal gets here. And you'll sleep on the sofa."

By the time Anne reached her house, she was jittery with nerves and fear and anger. Jake—she couldn't think of him by any name but Jake—had no right to come here like this. After all he'd done, he owed her peace and an illusion of safety.

But of course her safety was an illusion. It always had been. No matter how many promises the Marshals made to her, she'd never really believed they could protect her from her father.

The phone was ringing when she unlocked the door. She fastened the locks behind her and went to answer it. "How was coffee?" Maggie spoke with a musical lilt, her joy at having the scoop on Anne's love life—or so she thought—barely contained.

"Coffee was…tense." The Marshals had drilled into her that sticking as close to the truth as possible was the best way to keep from getting caught in a lie.

"I take it the two of you didn't part as friends."

"You could say that." She and Jake had grown so close in the weeks they'd spent together, but their final night had been all chaos and confusion. One moment they'd been dancing, her head cradled on his chest, wondering how soon they could make their excuses and head upstairs to bed. Nights in Jake's arms were heaven to her then. The next moment her world exploded in a hail of bullets and blood. Jake lay shattered on the dance floor, the front of her dress red with his blood. Her screams echoed over the music as two men she didn't recognize dragged her backward out of the room.

Later, still wearing the bloodied dress, huddled over a cup of bitter, cooling coffee in some gray-walled interrogation room, the agents had told her their version of the truth—that Jake West was really Jacob Westmoreland, accountant turned undercover FBI agent, assigned to infiltrate her family and bring down her father.

She hadn't hated him immediately. Hatred had come later, when the weight of his lies had settled on her. He'd told her he loved her. He'd said he wanted to protect her. He wanted them to get married, to live happily ever after. And all that time she hadn't even known his real name. How could anything else he'd said be true if his very identity had been a falsehood? He'd used her to betray her family. As much as she'd come to despise her father, she'd despised Jake almost as much.

"Are you going to tell me what happened?" Maggie asked. "'Cause if I want to talk to myself, I can do that without holding a phone to my ear."

Maggie must have been talking while Anne took her trip down memory lane. "Nothing happened," she said. "He said he was sorry. I said I was sorry, too. End of story."

"Uh-huh." Maggie sounded skeptical. "How long is he staying in town?"

"I don't know. Another day or two. We don't have plans." As soon as she got off the phone with Maggie, she'd need to call the number her WitSec handlers had given her. Denver was only five hours away—they could have someone here tomorrow, surely.

"He was really good-looking," Maggie said. "And I think he still has a thing for you. You have to admit, coming so far to say he was sorry took guts. Maybe you'll get together again while he's here."

"Maggie." Anne said her name as a warning.

Maggie laughed. "I know. I'm an incurable romantic. All right, I'll shut up about it. What are you doing tonight?"

"The usual. Schoolwork. Maybe some TV."

"Have a good night. See you tomorrow."

"Goodbye." Anne replaced the phone in the cradle and started to the kitchen to make tea. She was only halfway across the room when a knock on the door made her jump. She glanced out the window; the sky was a gray smudge against the black-and-white shadows of mountains, the day rendered in charcoal by the disappearing sun. Jake had said he would come by after dark—maybe a city boy used to all those lights thought this was dark enough.

She strode to the door and took a deep breath, bracing herself, then checked the peephole. She registered a man, about Jake's height, huddled in the shadows. Apparently, the bulb in her porch light had burned out. As long as Jake was here, she'd ask him to replace it. She threw back the chain, turned the dead bolt and jerked open the door.

A burly, dark-haired man shoved her back into the room and slammed the door behind him. He looked her up and down, his face expressionless. "Long time, no see, Elizabeth."

Chapter Five

Jake parked the rental car amid the jumble of vehicles at the auto-repair shop and began walking the few blocks toward Anne's house. The old joke about small towns rolling up the sidewalk when the sun set must be true; no one else was out and the only traffic was the occasional car on the central thoroughfare that connected with the state highway. Here on the side streets, it was as silent as a tomb. A quarter moon and the occasional glow from a porch light illuminated his path. The crunch of his footsteps on the unpaved shoulder of the road sounded too loud in the profound stillness.

For a man who'd spent all his life in the city, the silence felt vaguely threatening. He studied the shadows the trees and buildings cast, anticipating an ambush, but nothing moved.

He kept one hand wrapped around the gun in his coat pocket as he walked. Maybe he was being overly cautious and he and Anne had nothing to fear in this sleepy little town. But who was the man who'd been asking for her at the gym? Jake wouldn't leave her alone until he found out. He'd failed at protecting her from her father and his thugs before; he wouldn't let them near her again.

He approached the house from the back, though he doubted any of her neighbors were watching. He kept to the shadows along the side of the house, moving quickly toward the back steps. Maybe they should have agreed on some kind of signal, so she'd be sure it was him when he arrived. As he turned the corner toward the back of the house he froze, heart pounding.

The back door to Anne's house was open—not wide open, but cracked a few inches, sending a shaft of bright light onto a patch of trampled snow at the bottom of the steps. Jake drew the gun and sidestepped toward the door, keeping to the deepest shadows against the wall of the house. When he was sure the coast was clear, he took the steps two at a time, moving silently, and paused on the small landing at the top, holding his breath, listening.

"You don't remember me, do you?" The man's voice was nasal, the words clipped and staccato.

Anne's answer was unintelligible, but the terror in her voice made the hair on the back of Jake's neck stand on end. He nudged the door open a little wider with the toe of one shoe and leaned in.

"I worked for your father, but you never noticed me. You were too high and mighty to pay attention to the help."

Jake heard a scraping sound, as if someone had shoved a chair out of the way. He decided they were in the living room, just beyond the kitchen. Was it just Anne and this man, or had the intruder brought along help?

Jake slipped silently into the kitchen, keeping close to the wall, out of sight of the doorway between the kitchen and living room. "You deserve to die for what you did to your father," the man said.

"No!" Anne cried out and Jake rushed forward. He burst into the room and saw Anne struggling with a burly, dark-haired man. He aimed his pistol, but there was no way he could get off a clean shot without risking hitting Anne instead.

Anne's attacker wrapped one arm across her chest and pulled her against him, crushing her rib cage, lifting her off the ground. She writhed in his arms, kicking out. The man still didn't know Jake was in the room. That gave him a slim advantage, but he didn't yet see how to use it.

Anne kicked out, knocking over a table, on which sat a lamp. The glass base of the lamp shattered, and then the lightbulb exploded with a shower of sparks. Anne wailed—whether in pain or frustration, Jake didn't know, but the sound enraged him. He aimed the gun again, determined to get off a good shot.

Anne beat her fists against her assailant, who held her with one hand now while he groped in his jacket pocket, probably for a weapon. If he drew a gun, Jake would have to fire, and pray Anne was not in the way.

But just then, Anne leaned over and bit her attacker on the hand, hard enough to draw blood.

The man howled and released her, and Anne whirled and landed a solid punch on his chin. Her attacker reeled back, but in the same moment he drew a gun from his coat. It was the last move he ever made, as Jake shot him, twice, the impact of the bullets sending him sprawling across the back of the sofa.

Anne screamed, then stood frozen, her hands to her

mouth, her face the same bleached ivory color as the wall behind her. "Is there anyone else?" Jake asked.

She shook her head, still staring at the dead man draped across her sofa. Jake pocketed his gun and dragged the man onto the floor and laid him out on his back. He was a burly man in his forties, dressed in jeans and a flannel shirt and wearing a new-looking ski jacket, hiking boots and a knit cap. Anyone seeing him on the streets would have taken him for a local, or a visiting tourist.

Except most tourists didn't carry a Glock. Jake checked the weapon; it hadn't been fired. He slipped it into his other coat pocket and took out the man's wallet. "Robert Smith," he read the name on the driver's license.

"That's not his real name." Anne's voice was shaky, but surprisingly calm, considering she had a dead man laid out on her living room rug. "His name's DiCello. Some of my father's men called him Jell-O. He hated that."

"What's this on his jacket?" He tugged at a laminated tag hanging from the zipper pull of the jacket. "It's a lift ticket, from Telluride Ski Resort. Dated for yesterday." Had Mr. DiCello decided to take in a day on the slopes before driving over to Rogers to do a little business with his boss's estranged daughter?

The loud jangling of the phone surprised a cry from Anne, who immediately put a hand to her mouth, as if to hold back further cries. Jake stared at the ringing instrument. Had someone heard the shots? "You'd better answer it."

She nodded and picked up the phone. "Hello?"

She listened a moment, then forced a smile. "How

sweet of you, Mrs. Cramer, but everything's fine.... Yes, I heard it, too. It must have been a car backfiring."

She hung up the phone and looked at him. "The neighbor lady, checking on me."

"You did great." Better than great. She'd sounded perfectly calm and reasonable. As if thugs got shot up in her living room every night. "That was quite a punch you landed," he said.

She massaged the back of her hand—she'd likely have a bruise there tomorrow. "I've been taking boxing lessons. So I'd know how to defend myself. But it wouldn't have saved me. Not if you hadn't come along."

He moved toward her, intending to comfort her, but she stepped away from him, and hugged her arms tightly around her waist. He swallowed his disappointment. It didn't matter if she hadn't forgiven him; she still needed his help. "Your father's found you. You have to leave."

"Maybe my father didn't send him. Maybe he came on his own."

"Anne, look at me."

She met his gaze, and the anguish in her eyes cut him. He wanted to hold her close, to tell her again that he would protect her. But now wasn't the time. "You don't really believe this man, who you know works for your father, came here without your father's knowledge, do you?" he asked.

She shook her head. "No."

"Is there some place near here we can go that might be safe—just until we can make a plan?"

She straightened, visibly pulling herself together. "There are some cabins in the mountains about fifteen miles from here. The area is remote, on National Forest land. In the summer, a few people live there, but in the winter they're closed up. There's a gate over the road, but I know the combination to the lock."

She hadn't hesitated with her answer; she had all the details laid out. "You've been planning for something like this."

"I always knew I might have to leave. I didn't want to, but…" Her voice died, and her gaze dropped to the man at their feet.

"Pack a few things you'll need and we'll go. Now."

"What about him?"

"I'll drag him out back and hide the body under a pile of firewood. As cold as it is, it could be a long time before anyone finds him. If the police come looking for you, they might inadvertently lead your father to us."

"You think he'll send someone else after me?"

"You know he will."

She nodded. "Yes. What about the blood?"

"I'll clean it up. Now go."

Without another word, or a glance in his direction, she went into her bedroom and shut the door.

Jake stared at that shut door; it wasn't half as solid a barrier as the one she'd put around her heart. Fine. She could hate him all she wanted. Maybe he even deserved her hate. But that wouldn't stop him from protecting her. And it wouldn't stop him from finding the man who'd caused her so much pain, and making sure he could never hurt her again.

ANNE SHOVED UNDERWEAR, a change of clothes and a few cosmetics into an overnight bag. She added a phone charger and a box of ammunition. The thought of needing those bullets made her shake, but if forced, she would defend herself. She wouldn't hide behind Jake; she wouldn't trust her life to him alone.

Her own father wanted her dead. She'd accepted the truth of this intellectually, but in her heart she'd nurtured a kernel of hope that he would never follow through on his threats.

Tonight had destroyed that hope. If she let herself think too much about what had just happened, she might fall apart. So she clung to anger and nurtured that instead. A man had invaded her home—her sanctuary—and tried to destroy her. She wouldn't let that happen again.

Even if that meant depending on Jake in the short term. She needed him—and his gun—for protection right now. But as soon as she had a plan that would keep her safe, she'd say goodbye to him. She didn't need—or want—him in her life again. In his own way, Jake was as tied to violence as her father had been. The fact that he wanted revenge, even though he wasn't in law enforcement anymore, proved he was still a part of the violence. She was done with living that way, with danger and bloodshed as commonplace as Friday-night pizza or Sunday drives for other families.

When she emerged from the bedroom with the overnight bag and her coat, DiCello's body was gone. Jake had cleaned the floor and thrown a quilt over the back of the sofa to hide the bloodstains. "I've done the best I can," he said. "Are you ready?"

"Yes."

"We'll take my rental car. It's parked just down the street."

"What kind of car is it?" she asked.

"A Pontiac Vibe. What difference does that make?"

She shook her head. "It isn't four-wheel drive. We'll take my Subaru."

She could tell he wanted to argue. Jake liked to take charge, to have every situation under control. But this was her plan and she'd thought it out very carefully. "We'll need the four-wheel drive on the Forest Service roads," she said.

"Then give me your keys. I'll drive." He held out his hand.

She wrapped her hand more securely around the keys. "I know the way to the cabins and I'm a better driver in mountain snow than you are." And focusing on driving would keep her from brooding over the man who had attacked her, and the images of him dying right before her eyes. Though her father had been responsible for many deaths, the only other one she'd seen close up had been Jake. She moved past him, out the door.

She expected him to argue more, but he didn't, he merely slid into the passenger seat as she started the car. "You should call your friend Maggie, and tell her you're going out of town for a few days. Tell her your mom is sick or something."

"All right. I need to stop for gas. I'll call her then. And I'll call the U.S. marshal assigned to my case and let him know what's going on."

"Don't tell him you're with me."

"Why not?"

"I'm supposed to be retired. They'll see my presence as interfering."

"You *are* interfering." She gripped the steering wheel so tightly her fingers ached. "I was fine until you showed up."

"It was a coincidence that your father's goon showed up right after I did."

"A pretty big coincidence, if you ask me." She turned onto the main highway out of town. A few cars filled the parking spaces in front of the town's only bar, but there was no one outside to see her car glide past, or to wonder what the teacher was doing out so late.

"Where is this gas station?" He changed the subject.

"About five miles, by the lake. It's closed this time of night, but the electric pumps will take a credit card."

"I suppose we'll have to risk it. I'll stay out of sight of the security cameras, so it will look like you're alone."

"Why do I need to look like I'm alone?"

"If you're really on your way to visit your sick mother, why do you have a strange man with you?"

Right. She'd already forgotten the cover story he'd concocted. Not that she expected anyone to believe it. But maybe it would buy them a little time, and if anyone came around questioning Maggie, she'd have something to tell them.

Jake hid in the backseat while she fueled the car; then she parked around the side of the building, out of sight of the security cameras, and dialed Maggie's number. A sleepy voice answered on the fifth ring. "Hello?"

"Hello, Ty? I'm so sorry to bother you this late. This is Anne. May I speak to Maggie?"

"Sure, Anne. Everything all right?"

"It's fine. I just need to talk to Maggie a minute."

After a few seconds of fumbling with the phone, Maggie came on the line. "Anne, what's wrong?"

"I just learned my father is in the hospital in New York. I need to go up there and see him." She was surprised how smoothly the lie rolled off her tongue. She felt like an actress, delivering a line in a play.

"Oh, honey, I'm so sorry. What's wrong?"

"His heart. It…it doesn't look so good, I guess." Her father didn't have a heart where she was concerned, but as far as Anne knew, his health was fine.

"You never talked much about your parents before."

"My mother died when I was little." True. "My father and I aren't particularly close." Also true.

"I understand. You want to try to patch things up before it's too late. Don't worry about a thing. I'll call Mr. Strand first thing in the morning and explain."

Anne had been hoping to avoid a phone call to the principal. Lying to her best friend was bad enough; the more people she spoke with, the greater the chance of getting her story mixed up. "Thanks. I'll call you again when I know when I'll be home."

"Don't worry. Have you told Jake?"

"Jake?" She glanced at the man in the passenger seat and he sent her a questioning look. "Why would I tell Jake?"

"He's from New York, isn't he? He could fly back with you. Then you wouldn't have to be alone."

Maggie made it sound so romantic—the old flame comforting her in her time of need. In some ways, having Jake with her *was* comforting; at least he knew the truth about her. But she shouldn't trust him, and being with him complicated the situation even more. "I haven't seen Jake. He never knew my father, anyway." More lies. She hoped her friend would forgive her one day for her deception. Not that Anne would be around to accept that forgiveness. Now that her father had learned her identity, the Marshals office would give her a new one. If she kept this up, she wouldn't even remember who she was.

"I have to go now," she said. "I'll talk to you soon." She hung up before Maggie could ask more questions.

"Do you think you convinced her?" Jake asked.

"I think so." She scrolled through her phone directory until she found the number for U.S. Marshal Patrick Thompson.

He answered on the third ring, his voice as crisp and alert as if he'd been expecting her call. "Anne. Is something wrong?"

The concern in his voice brought a knot of tears to her throat. Marshal Thompson had always been kind, gentle even, treating her the way a caring big brother would look after his little sister. He'd done his best to make a horrible situation better, and the memory of that came rushing back at the sound of his voice. She struggled to rein in her emotions. Now was no time to break down. "One of my father's men, a man named DiCello, broke into my house tonight," she said. "He's dead and I'm leaving. I thought you'd want to know."

"Did he say how he found you? Did he say where your father is now?"

"No. We...we didn't talk much."

"You shot him?"

She hesitated, and looked again at Jake. "Yes." When they found the body, they'd probably figure out she'd lied; DiCello had been shot from behind, with a different gun from the one she owned—the gun Thompson himself had most likely given her. But none of that mattered now. "I'm headed to a place where I think I'll be safe, at least temporarily."

"Stay in touch and we'll send someone to get you. We'll set you up with a new identity."

"I'll call you tomorrow."

"I was going to contact you soon, anyway," he said. "To warn you that Jacob Westmoreland might try to get in touch."

"I…why would Jake…Jacob…be in touch? I mean, he's dead, isn't he?" She hoped he'd take her surprise at his mention of Jake as confusion.

"He was badly injured the night of the raid, but he didn't die. Apparently, he's been asking a lot of questions about you. He's been in contact with some friends at the Bureau."

"Why would he be asking questions about me?" She didn't look at Jake, but she could feel his eyes on her.

"You're sure the man who came after you tonight was from your father?"

"Yes. I knew him. He worked for my father." Why was Patrick changing the subject?

"Word is, Westmoreland is pretty upset about what happened. He's probably blames you for what happened to him and he may come after you, seeking revenge."

Chapter Six

Anne caught her breath, and almost dropped the phone. Patrick sounded so certain, and his words made sense: Jake had lost everything the night of the raid—his career, his bright future, and almost his life. If he thought she'd betrayed him to her father...

"I'll be careful," she said. "And I'll be in touch."

She disconnected the call, then switched off the phone and dropped it into her purse.

"Why did he ask you about me?" Jake asked.

She started the car and backed out of their parking spot. She had to remain calm and not let on that Patrick had warned her about him. "He heard you were looking for me. I told him I hadn't heard from you."

"Good girl."

The fact that he was so pleased by her deception made her even more nervous. What if Patrick had been telling the truth? So far, Jake had played the role of the wounded lover, but he'd been a good actor before, hadn't he? He'd fooled her father into trusting him. His love for her had felt real, but what did she know about love?

She didn't really know anything about Jake. When they'd been together before she'd only known the man he was pretending to be. Only later had she learned he worked for the FBI. She didn't know his real background, or what had happened to him during the months of his recovery.

She glanced at him as she turned the car onto the highway once more. He had his back to her, scanning the road for traffic. He was definitely different from the man she'd known before: he was less brash and more intense. Driven—by revenge? But revenge on her father, or on her?

"What have you been doing with yourself since you got out of rehab?" she asked, trying to keep the conversation light. If she kept Jake talking, maybe she could figure out his real motives for being here.

"I've spent most of my time looking for you."

That wasn't exactly reassuring. "Did you work, or… date?"

"I wasn't interested in dating, and looking for you was my work. I lived off my savings, and I was on disability pay for a while."

"You didn't think about maybe, I don't know, getting on with your life?"

"Not while I had unfinished business." She could feel his eyes on her in the dark.

She tightened her fingers around the steering wheel. She didn't like being afraid of Jake; it felt so wrong, since she'd once trusted him with her life.

"What do you think went wrong that day?" he asked.

"Wh-what do you mean?"

"I didn't have a clue your father suspected me. He never said anything, and he never tried to hide anything about the business from me."

"He never said anything to me, either," she said.

"If you'd known he planned to attack me, would you have warned me?"

"Yes!" She'd loved Jake more than she'd known it was possible to love a man. "I would have done anything for you. I thought you knew that."

"And now you just think I'm scum for lying to you."

"I don't know what to think, Jake. I gave everything to a man who didn't even exist. Can you understand how that might make me suspicious of your motives now?"

"I can understand. And I'm not asking you to pick up where we left off. But believe me when I say I want to help you and protect you."

"And you want revenge on my father."

"Only so he can't hurt you—and others—again."

She wanted to believe him. She wanted to believe that his feelings for her hadn't been lies. But a lot had happened to change both of them in the last year. Maybe in running away from her father's thugs, she was running into even worse danger with Jake.

An hour later, Anne hunched over the wheel of the Subaru wagon, easing it over frozen ruts in the Forest Service road, watching the thick wall of spruce and pine on either side of the narrow path for the gap that would indicate her turn onto an even narrower, less-used route. Clouds obscured the moon and the night was as black as a crow's wing. They hadn't passed another car since they'd turned off the main highway half an hour ago.

She'd decided she'd be cautious around Jake, but she wouldn't let fear get the better of her. She was armed, and McGarrity had taught her how to defend herself with her fists. She didn't have to be helpless, and that knowledge alone gave her power.

"Where are we, exactly?" Jake frowned at the darkness around them.

"We're in the Gunnison National Forest. In the summer it's a popular hiking and camping area."

"And in the winter?"

"In the winter the campgrounds are closed, the trails are usually covered in snow and the roads don't get much use." She pressed down on the gas and the car plowed through a snowdrift. It slid and fishtailed a little, but she steered it back onto firmer ground.

"When my handler from the Marshals office, Patrick Thompson, first showed me this car, I was horrified," she said. The green Subaru Outback was five years old and had clearly seen better days. Worse, it was a wagon, a vehicle for suburban moms and grandpas, not a fashionable young woman. In New York she'd had a BMW convertible, a silver Roadster she'd driven with the top down on all but the coldest, wettest days.

"This definitely isn't a car Elizabeth would have driven." Jake patted the dash. "But it suits Anne."

She sighed. "It does. Half the women in town, including most of the teachers, drive similar cars."

"It must have been very strange for you, starting over as someone else."

"It's still strange, but it got easier. When I first moved here, I put a coffee mug with my new name, Anne, on the table beside my bed, where I'd see it first thing every morning, to remind me I wasn't Elizabeth anymore. My name was Anne." She glanced at his profile in the darkness. His head was turned slightly and she knew he was watching her, but she couldn't make out his features, only the curve of his skull and the jut of his nose and chin, like one of those silhouette portraits that had been popular in Victorian parlors. "I spent my whole life until coming here trying to stand out, wanting to be noticed. I had to learn to do the opposite, to become invisible."

"I don't think you have to be invisible," he said. "You just have to blend in with your surroundings, to fit in context. You've done a good job of that. I might not have recognized you if I hadn't known what I was looking for."

"DiCello obviously didn't have any trouble, either." She spotted the break in the trees and slowed the car further. "There's our turn. We're almost there."

The steep, narrow drive was choked with snow. Anne gunned the car up the pitch, relaxing only when it leveled out in front of a gate formed by a single length of heavy pipe suspended across the road between two fat lodgepole pines. She set the brake and took a small flashlight from the console between the seats, then climbed out of the car. Jake followed.

"How do you know the combination?" he asked as he watched her dial the numbers into the lock on the chain that fastened one end of the pipe to a tree trunk.

"I came here with my camera to take pictures of the fall colors. You can't see it now, but there's a lovely little aspen next to this pine. Back in September it was covered in golden leaves. I took picture after picture of that tree, while the summer visitors packed up and left their cabins. I had a zoom lens focused in on this keypad, though no one ever suspected." The lock popped open and she unwound the chain. "My father had employees who used the same trick to steal people's ATM pin numbers. Wait here until I drive through, then replace the lock."

She drove past the gate, then waited while he swung the pipe over the road once more and refastened the lock. "Are you shocked, that I knew so much about my father's dirty dealings?" she asked as she drove on once more.

"You mean, would I rather think of you as an unsullied innocent who had no idea her father was a thief and drug dealer and pimp and murderer? I don't think anyone can live for years in a world of crime and not be touched by it, and that includes me."

She hadn't been unsullied or innocent, but she'd perfected the art of looking the other way, and of telling herself the things her father did were none of her business, that they didn't matter to her. Jake had made her see things differently. She couldn't be grateful to him for that, not when it had destroyed the only life she'd known, and taken away the only family she had.

The cabins sat in a rough semicircle amid the trees, separated from each other by several hundred yards and piles of boulders that rose almost to the roofs. There were five; she chose the smallest, the farthest from the road. Even in summer it had been closed up tight. Unused.

She parked the car behind a screening stack of boulders and they climbed out. It was after midnight, and the cold was like a slap, hard and stinging. Anne led the way to the door and felt for the key above the lintel. Jake took it from her and unlocked the door and pushed it open.

The cabin smelled of stale ashes and dust. Jake fumbled along the wall by the door and she laughed. "There's no light switch," she said. "No electricity." She scanned the area with her flashlight beam until she spotted a kerosene lantern sitting on a table next to a box of kitchen matches. She lit the lantern and turned down the wick. Its golden glow illuminated the small main room, which consisted of a kitchen area, a table and two chairs and a worn love seat and armchair.

Jake opened the door on the far side of the room and looked in. "Bedroom," he announced, then checked the second door on an adjacent wall. "Bathroom—or at least a toilet and sink."

"The water's probably shut off for the winter so the pipes don't freeze," she said. She turned her attention to the empty woodstove that squatted between the front room's two windows. "There should be some firewood out back," she said.

He left, and returned with an armload of wood. She laid a fire, building a bed of small sticks and crumpled paper, then adding split pieces of wood. When she touched a match to the paper, it caught, and smoke curled up the chimney. After she was sure the fire was blazing, she closed the stove door. "It will be warmer in a little bit."

"I'm impressed," he said. "Were you a Girl Scout?"

"I've learned a lot of things since coming here." The instinct to survive was a powerful teacher. She made sure the curtains were pulled shut over the windows, then checked the contents of the two cupboards in the kitchen. "There's coffee and hot chocolate, and some canned soup and stews. We won't starve."

"Do you know who owns this cabin?" Jake asked. He slid onto a stool at the small breakfast bar.

She filled a kettle from a ten-gallon bottle of water on a stand beside the old-fashioned round-top refrigerator. The refrigerator was propped open by sticks held in place with bungee cords. "According to the county land records, it belongs to a man in Minneapolis. He inherited it from his parents. I don't think he comes down here very often—the cabin was empty every time I checked this last year."

"And the other cabins?"

"They belong to summer people. That's what everyone around here calls them. They live somewhere else and they come here every summer for a few weeks to hang out in nature."

"But we're on Forest Service land?"

"That's right." She lit a burner on the gas stove. "The cabins were here before the land was taken as National Forest, so the families were allowed to keep them and use them, but they're not allowed to make any changes without government approval—so no insulation, no electricity, no modernization, except ten years or so ago they made everyone fill in their outhouses and install flush toilets. Water comes from cisterns or a pump dropped in the creek down there."

"A creek that is frozen this time of year."

"Right. So we won't be using the indoor toilet. The cabins weren't designed for winter use, only as summer retreats."

"How did you ever find this place?" he asked.

"I came hiking with Maggie and her husband, Ty, not too long after I moved here. She told me all about the cabins. A few weeks later I came back on my own to check them out."

"And you brought your camera."

"I thought it would be a good idea to have a plan—someplace to go if I needed to hide. Even in the summer many of the cabins are empty, but if someone had asked,

I could have posed as a friend of the guy who owns the cabin, using it for the weekend, or something like that."

"That was good thinking. But then, I'm not surprised. You were always one of the smartest people I knew."

She busied herself finding cups and spooning cocoa into them, afraid if she looked at him he would see how pleased she was by the compliment, and how uncomfortable that made her now. It reminded her too much of one of the things she had loved about him, before: he didn't think that because she was beautiful, she was dumb. The other men in her life—her father and brother and her father's friends—dismissed women as empty-headed dolls.

"What's the rest of the plan now that we've made it here?" he asked.

She poured boiling water over the cocoa and slid a cup toward him. "I suppose I wait for Patrick—Marshal Thompson—to take me someplace new where I can start over again."

"Does that bother you?" He looked thoughtful as he stirred the cocoa. "I mean, how many times will you have to start over before you forget who you are? Or before your father stops looking for you?"

"My father will never stop looking." He could make all the speeches he wanted about her being dead to him, but until she was actually dead, and he had proof of it, her betrayal would eat at him like a cancer. "I've heard that hate is another side of love. As much as my father loved me, I think he hates me that much now." She would be his obsession, as other enemies had been. He had destroyed the others, every one. He wouldn't let her be his one failure. "The Marshals tell me they can protect me, that they've protected thousands of other people."

"They haven't done a very good job keeping you hidden so far," he said.

"No. You found me."

"I'm not the one you have to worry about."

Patrick hadn't been so sure about that. He thought Jake was out for revenge; maybe so, but he seemed willing to keep her safe as long as he thought she might help him find her father. "The problem with the Marshals is that too many people know who I am and where I am. They can talk about how secure their system is, but there are always leaks."

"True. But what other choice do you have?"

"I could head out on my own, go to Denver or Los Angeles or some other big city. I can buy a passport with another name and leave the country."

"You know how to get a fake passport?" He sounded skeptical. "But then, I guess you are your father's daughter."

"Don't judge me. I know how to do what I need to do to stay alive."

"I wasn't judging you." His tone softened. "You have another choice."

"What's that?"

"Work with me to find your father. See him arrested again and locked up for good. With him out of the picture, you'll be safe. You won't have to hide."

She stirred the chocolate, the spoon hitting the side of the cup with a tinkling melody. "He escaped before. He can escape again."

"There's something you ought to know about his

escape," he said. "Something I uncovered in my research that was hushed up at the time. Maybe knowing the whole story will help you make up your mind."

Chapter Seven

Anne glared at him, anger growing. "Jake, I'm tired and I'm stressed and I don't like playing games," she said. "If you have something to say, come straight out with it."

"First, tell me what you were told about your father's escape."

"Patrick met with me in person, before it was even in the news." She'd only been in Rogers a month then, so he'd arranged to meet her in a mall in Grand Junction, where they'd purchased tickets to an afternoon matinee, then ducked into an empty auditorium. "He told me my father's lawyers petitioned for a transfer to a different prison unit. No one in law enforcement expected the request to be granted—my father was too much of a risk. But the transfer was granted. The officers transporting him to the new facility were ambushed and overwhelmed and my father got away. By the time authorities discovered what had happened, hours had passed and there was no trace of my father."

"It all sounds very convenient, doesn't it?" Jake asked. "At the very least, it sounds as if someone paid off the judge to grant the transfer, and then pulled other strings to delay the reporting of the escape."

"Patrick said it took place in a remote area. They thought my father got away via helicopter."

"Did he also tell you the FBI suspected your father had help from higher up?"

"Higher up? What do you mean?"

"I don't have any proof, but my friends in the Bureau tell me they think a prominent politician pulled strings and paid off some guards to look the other way."

"Because my father paid him?" Sam had said once that he could make anyone do what he wanted if he waved enough money under their nose.

"Either that or he was connected to Sam in some way that he didn't want to come out."

"Maybe so," she said. "But how is knowing this going to help me decide whether to go back into Wit-Sec or stay and help you?"

"Because my friends in the Bureau say they're closing in on the people who helped Sam escape. They're going to make an arrest soon. Your father won't have so many friends to rely on next time."

She shook her head. "You make it sound so simple. But I don't have any idea where my father is."

"I think he's near here. I don't think DiCello had to travel all that far to find you in Rogers." He reached into his pocket and took out a piece of paper. She recognized the lift ticket that had been on DiCello's coat. "This is from Telluride. Dated yesterday," Jake said.

"Maybe DiCello stole the coat."

"Or maybe he went skiing. Does your father ski?"

She hesitated. She didn't want Jake to be right; she didn't want her father to be so close. "Yes. Every winter when I was a kid we took a family ski vacation." For one week every winter they'd been like any other family, renting a condo, riding up the lifts together, racing down the mountains. They drank cocoa and went for sleigh rides and gathered around bonfires. Just like ordinary people, as long as you ignored the beefy bodyguards who accompanied her father everywhere. When they were very young, her mother had taught Anne and her brother to call the men "uncle." Uncle Ramon and Uncle Frankie and Uncle Tiva. Four-year-old Sammy had asked once why there were so many uncles but no aunts, and her father had repeated the joke over and over for weeks, always to uproarious laughter.

"Did you ever come to Telluride?" Jake asked.

She shook her head. "Mostly we went to Europe or Canada. Once to California, but never Colorado."

"Getting out of the country might be tough for your father right now. He's at the top of the FBI's Ten Most Wanted list. Does he know anyone in Telluride? Any friends?"

"I don't know. He had connections all over the country. All over the world."

"Search your memory. Maybe he's combining a little vacation with business."

The business of hunting down his own daughter. She shuddered.

"Do you have any idea how DiCello knew where you were?" he asked.

"I've been thinking about that." She pushed aside the cooling cocoa. "Maggie told me my picture was on the front page of the Telluride paper yesterday. I was helping with a fundraising booth at the Winter Carnival and a reporter took a picture without my knowledge. Someone who knew me before might have recognized me."

"I think that's a pretty strong indication that your

father is in Telluride. It's not that far from here, right? I saw a brochure at my hotel in Rogers."

"It's about an hour away. But all that lift ticket tells us was that DiCello was in Telluride. Maybe he was on vacation."

"We could go there tomorrow and find out."

"I'm supposed to call Patrick tomorrow. We're going to arrange to meet somewhere."

"You can meet him in Telluride."

She opened her mouth to say no—to tell him she didn't care if her father was in Telluride or Timbuktu. But as much as she could lie about other things, she couldn't lie to herself. Not about this. She wanted to know if her father was nearby; she needed to know.

"Maybe I could arrange to meet Patrick in Telluride."

"We can go in the morning. When are you supposed to check in with Thompson again?"

"We didn't set a time."

"Then leave your phone off and call him when we reach Telluride. After we've had a chance to look around."

He didn't press or plea, just waited for the answer he probably already knew she would give. "All right," she said. "I can do that."

He looked around the cabin. "We should be safe enough alone here tonight."

His words were innocent enough, but they struck a chord deep inside her. The last time she'd spent the night alone with Jake they'd been lovers. They'd slipped away to his apartment and celebrated like honeymooners, oblivious to the rest of the world and its problems.

Only two days later that world had come crashing down around them. They weren't the same people they'd been in that apartment so long ago—how could they be? But the memory of all she'd felt for him rose up in her. She didn't love Jake anymore—she couldn't, after the way he'd lied to her, and all he'd put her through. But that didn't stop her from wanting that kind of love again. She just needed to remember the difference between the fantasy and the reality and not make the mistake of confusing the two.

"You take the bed," he said. "I can bunk on the sofa."

"All right." The sofa was really a love seat, too short for him. He'd be pretty uncomfortable, but it wouldn't kill him for one night. In the morning they'd drive to Telluride and find nothing to alarm them. She'd call Patrick and arrange to meet him somewhere nearby. She'd say goodbye to Jake and probably never see him again. The thought brought a lump to her throat and she had to turn away.

JAKE HAD GIVEN ANNE a lot to mull over and she was obviously upset—not to mention dealing with the shock that someone had really tried to kill her, which was probably just now beginning to hit her. "Give me the keys and I'll get your overnight bag from the car," he said. She'd probably appreciate a few moments alone to pull herself together.

Stepping outside was like stepping into a cave—dark and bitingly cold. Trees blocked the stars, and there probably wasn't another occupied house for miles in any direction. He stood on the steps of the cabin, allowing his eyes to adjust to the darkness and listening to his own breathing. He had never been anywhere so dark and silent and remote.

Click. The sound, like metal striking against a stone,

rang loud in the stillness. Jake froze, one hand on the switch of the flashlight he'd brought from the cabin, the other on the gun in his pocket. Nothing.

He waited, until his feet grew numb and he could no longer feel his nose, but he heard nothing. Maybe an animal had made the noise, or the wind rubbing tree branches together. Moving slowly, placing each foot silently in the snow, he made his way to the car. He switched on the flashlight and aimed the beam low, shielding it with his body. The beam illuminated a confusion of footprints in the snow—his and Anne's steps, when they'd arrived at the cabin.

When he opened the car door the dome light came on. He crouched down behind the door, trying to stay out of sight of anyone who might be watching. Of course, no one was out there, but he couldn't shake the sensation that he wasn't alone.

He retrieved Anne's bag from the backseat, then opened the glove box and pulled out a map of Colorado. He wanted to study it, to figure out where they were now, and to determine the best route to Telluride tomorrow.

He switched off the flashlight and slammed the car door, plunging himself into darkness once more. Retracing his steps to the front door by memory, he opened and shut the door, but remained outside. Then he stood very still, waiting in the deepest shadows beside the steps.

He counted off a full three minutes before he heard the faint crunch of footsteps in the snow, the creak of a car door opening and the quiet *thunk* of it closing again. Then an engine roared to life. None of the sounds were close—the car was probably a quarter of a mile away or more. Sound carried farther out here in this profound silence.

"Jake?" A strip of light fell across the snow as the door to the cabin opened a few inches and Anne peered out. "Jake, are you all right?"

"I'm fine." He stepped out to where she could see him.

"What have you been doing out here so long?" she asked.

He debated whether to tell her; he could worry enough for both of them. But maybe she'd have a simple explanation for the sounds—a neighbor he didn't know about or something like that.

"Let me come inside and I'll tell you," he said. "I'm frozen."

She opened the door to let him in. He dropped her bag on the table, then stripped off his coat and stood in front of the fire, warming his hands. "I thought I heard something," he said.

"What, exactly?"

"Someone walking around out there—not too far away, maybe up by the road. I pretended to go inside, then I stood in the dark and waited. After a few minutes, I heard footsteps again, then a car door opening and someone driving away."

She frowned. "What time is it now?"

He slipped his phone from his pocket and checked the display. "Twelve minutes after one."

"Kids come out here to party sometimes, but not in the winter, and not on a weeknight," she said. "And when we drove in, I didn't see any sign that anyone else had been here, not since the last snow at least."

"Maybe I should walk up to the road and check."

He didn't relish the idea of venturing out into that cold blackness again, but he would if he had to.

"And then what?" She began to pace, arms folded across her chest. "So someone drove in here, then turned around and drove out. It might not mean anything."

"Or it might mean you were followed."

"I wasn't followed. I was watching and I'm sure of it. And if someone had followed and they wanted to harm us, why leave, having done nothing?"

"I'll feel better checking."

"Fine. Go check."

"I don't like the idea of leaving you here alone." Maybe whoever it was wanted to lure him away, so they could get to Anne when she was more vulnerable.

She stopped in front of him. "Well, I'm not going out there with you," she said. "It doesn't make sense to me to go stumbling around in the dark in the freezing cold instead of staying in this nice warm cabin behind locked doors. We're bound to be more vulnerable outside than in."

He nodded. Leaving shelter didn't make sense, especially with no obvious assailant. "You're right. It was probably just someone who was lost or something. I can check in the morning."

"Good. I found some sheets and blankets in the bedroom closet, and a pillow you can use."

He took the items, though he doubted he'd sleep. He'd sit up and keep watch. "Try to get some rest," he said.

"You, too." She started to turn away, then turned back and added, "I'm glad you were with me tonight. Not only because you saved my life, but because I'm glad I don't have to do this alone. That was always the worst part, when I was making my plan—knowing I'd be running away alone, with no one to tell me I was doing the right thing, that I wasn't crazy or paranoid."

"You're not crazy or paranoid. And I'm glad I'm with you, too." As horrible as the events of this day had been, the one good thing was that he'd been able to help her. He'd begun to make up for the way he'd let her down before.

ANNE WAS TOO EXHAUSTED, emotionally and physically, to change into a nightgown, so she crawled into bed in her clothes. She expected to lie awake, worrying about whoever had been in that car up near the road, and about where Patrick planned to send her next, and where sticking with Jake might lead. But weariness won out over worry, and she fell into a fitful sleep.

She awoke to pitch darkness, and the disorienting feeling of not knowing where she was. She stared into the darkness, awareness slowly returning, and the memory of the man who had attacked her at her home in Rogers. She didn't like to think what would have happened if Jake hadn't shown up when he did.

Something tickled her nose, and she sneezed. Then she sat bolt upright, fear making her heart pound. The smell of smoke filled the room, and she heard the unmistakable crackle of flames. "Jake!" she shouted as she threw back the covers and shoved her feet into her boots. "Jake, wake up! The cabin's on fire!"

Chapter Eight

Anne groped her way to the bedroom door and pressed both palms against the wood. The door was warm—too warm. Local firefighters had given a fire safety talk at the school earlier this year. She remembered their warning to never open a warm door in a fire, that doing so could send the flames rushing into the room. If the door was warm, you were supposed to find a window and escape that way.

But Jake was on the other side of that door. The love seat where he slept was near the woodstove, where the fire had likely started. Had he awakened in time and fled out the front door—or was he already dead, overcome by smoke? She pushed the thought away and hurried to the window. She'd go around to the front of the cabin and try to reach Jake that way. Or maybe she'd find him outside, safe and trying to reach her.

She tugged hard at the window, until it opened with a screeching protest. Bitterly cold air rushed in—air that might feed the fire and engulf the bedroom. She started to climb out, then reached back and yanked the heavy wool blanket off the bed. Maybe she could use it to beat out flames, or as an extra layer of protection if she had to go in after Jake.

Dragging the blanket behind her, she jumped out the window and made her way through the snow to the front of the cabin. The brilliant glow of the blaze momentarily blinded her as she rounded the corner of the house. She shaded her eyes with one hand, and stumbled on, but when she reached the front of the house, she drew back, gasping. The entire front wall of the cabin was ablaze, flames licking at the windows and door, and swiftly devouring the wooden shingles of the roof. "Jake!" she screamed above the roar of the inferno.

No answer came to her cries, and she saw no sign of him in the area illuminated by the fire. He must still be inside. Reaching him through the front door would be impossible. But the side walls remained intact. There was a chance she might get to him through the window. Still dragging the blanket, she ran back the way she'd come, and stopped at the window that opened into the cabin's main room. The sash refused to yield to her tugging, so she raced to the wood pile, grabbed a length of stove wood and ran back and swung it at the window, shattering the glass. Then she draped the blanket across the sash and boosted herself inside.

The flames that engulfed the front of the cabin illuminated a cavern of swirling smoke and shadows. "Jake!" she shouted.

Harsh coughing answered her. "Over here!" said a hoarse voice.

She wrapped herself in the blanket and shuffled toward the voice, trying to hold her breath, but unable to avoid the choking smoke. "Jake!" she called again, and began to cough.

"Here!"

She stumbled forward once more and almost fell over

him. He pulled her down beside her. "Stay low. The air is better down here."

Not much better that she could tell, but now wasn't the time to argue. She handed him a corner of the blanket. "Use this to shield your face. We've got to get to the window."

"I was trying to get to you in the bedroom, but I couldn't find the door in the smoke and darkness."

"Don't talk. Just move."

Together, they crawled across the floor, toward where she hoped the window was situated. A current of colder air told her they were getting close, so she stood, and helped Jake to stand also. They rushed to the window and half jumped, half fell onto the snow outside.

They lay side by side, wrapped in the singed blanket and gasping for breath. She felt Jake's hand, heavy on her back. "Are you...all right?" he gasped.

"I'm fine. The smell of smoke must have woken me and I climbed out the bedroom window."

"I planned to sit up all night, keeping watch, but I must have drifted off. I didn't wake up until the front wall was on fire. By then the smoke was so thick, and I was disoriented." He raised himself up on his elbows and looked at her. "I don't think I'd have made it if you hadn't come after me."

"I couldn't leave you." She blinked, trying to hold back a sudden flood of stinging tears. She'd been alone so long. Jake was the first person in a year who really knew her story, who had some inkling of what she was going through. For that reason alone, she couldn't turn her back on him, not yet.

He sat and helped her to sit, too. "Should we call 9-1-1?" she asked.

"With what? My cell phone is in the cabin."

"Mine, too. And my purse and, oh no—the car keys."

"I have the keys." He pulled them from his pocket. "I must have automatically stuck them in my pants when I came back from getting your bag."

A section of the cabin roof collapsed in a shower of sparks and she flinched. Even from a distance of ten yards, she could feel the intense heat of the blaze. "I hope it doesn't spread to the other cabins," she said.

"I don't think it will." He stood and offered her his hand. She grasped it and pulled herself up. "This cabin is set away from the others, and there's no wind. I think when the fuel—the cabin—is gone, the fire will burn itself out."

"I don't understand what happened," she said. "I checked the woodstove before we went to bed and everything seemed fine. But I guess all it takes is one spark—"

"The fire didn't start from the woodstove," he said.

She stared at him. "Then how?"

"Come on." He grabbed her hand and urged her toward the front of the cabin. "The fire started in the front."

She nodded. "The whole front wall was burning— that's why I had to come through the window on the side."

"For a whole wall to burn like that, so quickly, blocking the main exit, I'd think it would take some kind of accelerant."

"You mean—someone deliberately set the fire? But who? How?" She looked around, fighting rising panic. She'd chosen this place because it was safe. Now he was telling her danger had followed her even here?

"Look." He pointed to twin lines of tire tracks in the snow. "They weren't here earlier, I'm sure."

"But you heard a car earlier, and footsteps."

"Maybe the same people, checking to make sure we were here. They waited until we fell asleep and came back. Or maybe there was no connection at all."

She stared at the tracks, anger quickly overtaking panic. "You think someone planned the fire, knowing we were the ones in the cabin?"

"Yes, but they probably haven't gone far. They'll be back soon, to make sure the fire did its job."

"They must have followed us here."

"If they did, they're much better at tailing someone than anyone I've ever seen. I was watching and I never saw anyone, and you didn't either. On these deserted roads, any other vehicle would stand out."

"They couldn't have known I'd be here. I never told anyone—not even Maggie."

"We can't worry about how they found you right now. The point is, they did. And we have to leave before they come back."

"You're right." She headed toward the car. He put his hands on her shoulders and steered her toward the passenger side. "I'll drive."

She didn't argue. She was too shaken to face negotiating the narrow, snow-choked Forest Service road. She hoped Jake was up to the task; she had no idea what kind of driver he was. In New York, they'd taken taxis or the subway, or her father had sent one of his drivers to take them wherever they needed to go. She kept her convertible for weekend trips upstate or to the coast.

"Is there another way out of here?" he asked as

he started the car. "I meant to check the map, but I never did."

"You have to take this road up to the gate, but there you can turn right instead of left and take another series of forest roads that come out near a little town called New Richmond. It's a lot farther back to the highway than the way we came in."

"We'll take it. I don't want to risk running head-on into the arsonist on these narrow pig trails."

At the gate, he stopped and waited for her to dial in the combination, but she'd only taken a few steps from the car when she saw there was no need. The chain hung loose, the lock lying in the snow. She forced herself to move forward and swing open the gate, then closed it and climbed in the car again. "Someone cut the lock off," she said.

"Whoever followed us didn't have the combination."

She hugged her arms across her chest and shivered. "We'll buy coats in Telluride," he said. "Meanwhile, turn the heater up."

"It's not the weather making me cold," she said. "I just can't believe someone followed us—and tried to burn us to death."

"I'm guessing they think two accidental deaths would be easier to deal with than two obvious murders."

"They weren't very smart," she said. "An arson investigator would have spotted the accelerant."

"Maybe. Maybe not. We don't know what they used."

"And we don't know who they are."

"Except they probably work for your father."

"Maybe. Maybe not."

"Do you have other enemies?"

"No. Do you? Maybe we're looking at this wrong.

Maybe they're not after me at all. If my father knew you were still alive, he'd be very happy to see you dead." The idea that Jake might be the target of her father's wrath—that Sam Giardino might not even know anything about her—flooded her with relief. Not that she wanted Jake to be in danger, but she dreaded starting life over with yet another new name and profession.

"I don't think you're right," Jake said.

"You don't know that I'm wrong."

"All right. I'll concede it's a possibility that whoever set the fire was after me, and you were only a secondary target—a bonus. That still leaves us with the same problem. Until your father is behind bars again, neither one of us is safe."

"He was behind bars before—I testified to put him there. But he didn't stay there for long." Despair had engulfed her when Patrick had told her of her father's escape from prison. She'd given up everything in order to see him convicted; his escape made her sacrifice worth nothing.

"He'll stay there this time. The authorities won't risk being made to look like fools twice."

"People will do a lot of foolish things when confronted with the kind of money and power my father can offer."

He fell silent, negotiating a particularly bad section of road. Anne clenched her teeth, and prayed they wouldn't end up stuck in a snowdrift here in the middle of nowhere, with an unknown assailant out to silence them.

She let out a sigh of relief as Jake turned onto a slightly wider, smoother section of road.

"You're right," he said. "I can't guarantee your father

won't get out of prison again. But if we do nothing, he definitely won't be arrested, and he'll continue to do everything in his power to see that both of us are dead. You can go back into witness protection and hope he doesn't find you again, but he's already beat the system once."

Denying his words wouldn't make them any less true. And if she ran away again, without even trying to change things, she'd have one more thing to regret. "All right," she said. "I'll do what I can to help. But only for a few days. I can't give you any more time than that."

"And I won't ask for any more."

His words should have made her feel relieved; instead, they filled her with sadness. That's what she got for thinking about regrets. Surely she would regret the love she and Jake had had, and could never regain, for the rest of her life.

"Patrick told me I should be careful of you," she said.

"Oh? When did he tell you that?"

"When I talked to him last night. He said you'd been asking about me and he thought you were looking for revenge."

"I am looking for revenge, but on your father, not you."

"I know that now."

"How do you know that?"

"Setting a fire that you almost died in would be a pretty stupid way to try to do away with me."

"Thanks for agreeing that I'm not stupid."

"You're stubborn and reckless—but not stupid." And the same might have been said of her, once upon a time, back when she was daring Elizabeth, not quiet and cautious Anne.

"*Nil opus captivis*. Do you still believe that?" he asked.

The idea of doing whatever she had to in order to get what she wanted had appealed to her when she was a young, spoiled socialite, to whom very little had ever been denied. From the perspective of a woman who had paid the price for that kind of ruthlessness, the words she'd once had tattooed on the base of her spine struck her as a sick joke. "I'm ashamed I thought those words were important," she said.

"We're both a little older and I hope a lot wiser now," he said. "Suffering and loss make you understand what's really important in life."

But what if the really important things—love and home and family—were all the things you had lost? "What's important to you?" she asked.

"Right now, what's important is seeing that your father is back behind bars, where he can never hurt anyone else again."

So revenge was most important to Jake—not home or family or love. For all he'd suffered after her father's attack, he didn't value the things that were most precious to her. She shouldn't have been surprised, really. How could a man who had made a living out of lying and pretending to be someone he was not ever be happy with simple truths?

She had to remember that, for all her strong feelings for Jake, she hadn't really loved him. She'd only loved a mirage he'd created to fool her. The man she loved didn't exist, and he never would.

AN HOUR BEFORE DAWN, Jake stopped the car at the intersection of the Forest Service road and the highway. True darkness had receded, and the trees along the side of the road looked like black smudges against a gray sky. They hadn't seen another car since leaving the burning cabin; maybe they'd lost whoever had been tracking them. "Which way do I turn?" he asked.

Anne pointed right. "Telluride is that way."

"How are you holding up?" he asked. Her hair was disheveled and she wore the same clothes she'd had on last night, reeking of smoke. She had to be tired and hungry, yet she hadn't made one complaint. He couldn't imagine Elizabeth enduring such discomfort gracefully. She'd been used to living like a princess and taken for granted she should be treated like one.

With all that finery and privilege stripped away, Jake could see that Anne was made of stronger stuff.

"I'm fine." She offered a weary smile. "Before we reach Telluride, we'll go through New Richmond."

"What's in New Richmond?"

"Not much. But there's a convenience store where we can stop for gas and coffee, and to clean up a little." She leaned forward and touched his cheek. "You've got a smudge of soot."

The gesture was innocent; she'd leaned back and was looking out the car window again almost before he'd realized what was happening. But the sensation of her cool fingers against his cheek lingered, calling forth all the other times she'd touched him, sometimes not so innocently.

Enough, he cautioned himself, and he turned the car right onto the highway. He needed Anne's help to find her father, and he wanted to protect her, but he shouldn't waste time trying to recreate something that had been built on lies and fantasy. They both lived in a harsher, if more honest, world now.

Half an hour later, he pulled the car alongside the gas pumps at the Gas and Ready in New Richmond. She went inside while he filled the car, and then he made his way to the men's room, where he did his best with soap and paper towels to make himself look presentable. He needed a shave and a change of clothes, but this would have to do.

When he emerged from the restroom, she was waiting. She handed him a cup of coffee. "Do you still drink it black?" she asked.

He nodded. She'd washed the last of the makeup from her face and pulled her hair back into a sleek ponytail. She looked very young and vulnerable. The thought that someone out there was trying to kill her made him shaky with anger.

"They have breakfast sandwiches, too," she said. "And we should get these." She handed him a dark blue bundle of cloth.

He set his cup on the counter and unfolded a thick sweatshirt, and read the slogan printed on the front. *Telluride—Higher, Steeper, Deeper.*

"I got this one for me." She held up a pink shirt, printed with the words *Official Ski Bunny.*

"I guess this will help us look like tourists," he said.

"At least we'll be warmer, and have one thing that doesn't smell like smoke."

He paid for their purchases, thankful he'd still had his wallet and credit cards when he'd crawled from the burning cabin. "We'll get a room in Telluride and shower." He rubbed his sandpapery chin. "And I need to shave."

"I hope you have a big expense account for this little expedition." She settled into the passenger seat and fastened her seat belt. "Hotel rooms in Telluride don't come cheap."

"I think I can manage." He'd remained at full pay all the months he'd been recuperating, the money piling up in the bank with no way for him to spend it. And he had savings; he didn't care if he had to spend every penny to make sure Sam Giardino ended up back behind bars.

"We'll need some more clothes, too. Those won't be cheap, either." They turned onto the highway once more, the view of snowcapped mountains against the pink clouds of sunrise worthy of any tourist postcard. "Telluride used to be a sleepy little hippie hangout," she said. "But now it's home to the rich and famous."

And the infamous, he hoped. "We have to have new clothes," he agreed. "It's pretty hard to sneak up on someone when you reek like a campfire."

"Good point. I know a chichi thrift store on the main drag that won't break your bank."

He laughed.

"What's so funny?"

"Elizabeth would have never shopped at a thrift store," he said.

"Elizabeth's dead. You need to remember that." The finality of her words sent a chill through him. Of course Elizabeth was dead. And he was after the man who had destroyed her. The loss had been a tragic one, though he couldn't help thinking now that maybe the woman beside him was stronger and wiser than the pretty, naive socialite he'd once loved.

They drove on in silence. Maybe she was as mired in thoughts of the past and what might have been as he was. But after a few miles he became aware that they weren't alone on the highway anymore. He checked the rearview mirror and saw a black SUV, windows heavily tinted to prevent any view of driver or passengers, approaching at a fast clip. "We might be in for trouble," he said.

"What is it?"

"I think we're being followed, and this time they're not even trying to hide it."

Chapter Nine

Anne stared at the black vehicle barreling toward their car. It was driving much too fast for the narrow, winding highway, but the driver expertly negotiated the sharp curves, and the powerful engine appeared to manage the steep grades without strain. "Are you sure they're after us?" she asked.

"No, I'm not sure." Jake pulled his gun from beneath his shirt and laid it on the console between them. "But there's no one else out this time of morning, and I don't like the looks of them. If they pass us by, no harm done, but I want to be ready."

"Of course." There was something sinister about the vehicle, with its blacked-out windows and swift approach. She glanced to the side of the road, where the world fell away into a steep, rocky canyon. On Jake's side of the car, sheer rock walls rose beside the road. They were stuck on the side of a mountain, with a swiftly approaching enemy who would probably like nothing better than to knock them off into the abyss below.

"They won't shoot us," she said. "They'll try to make it look like an accident. They'll try to run us over the side."

"I think so." He gripped the steering wheel with both hands, and constantly shifted his gaze from the road to the rearview mirror and back. "I'm going to do my best to keep that from happening."

"What do you need me to do?" she asked.

"Tighten your seat belt, and if they start shooting, duck."

"I could try to shoot at them."

"Don't waste ammunition unless they get really close."

She picked up the pistol and checked that there was a bullet in the chamber. "Have you shot much before?" he asked.

"After I came to Rogers, someone sent me a gun in the mail. I think it was probably Patrick, though he wouldn't admit to it."

"Your father didn't teach you to shoot?"

"Absolutely not. Women weren't supposed to concern themselves with that sort of thing. That's what the muscle was for."

"What did you do with the gun Thompson sent you?"

"I took it to the local shooting range and practiced, but firing at a moving vehicle is a lot different from hitting a target on the range."

"It is. But if they succeed in running us off the road and then come after us, you might be able to hit one of them."

"If they run us off this road, I don't think either one of us will be shooting anyone." She took in the steep drop-off to her right and shuddered.

"Good point." The Subaru sped up and the passing scenery became a blur of gray rock, blue sky and white snow. Anne clutched the armrest and bit her lip to keep from crying out as they careened around one hairpin turn after the next, all the while steadily climbing the mountain. The screech of protesting brakes tore into the early morning silence as the SUV followed, skidding around the turns. "He's got a higher center of gravity," Jake said. "He can't corner as well as we can."

His logical analysis of such an emotionally charged situation made her feel calmer. But then, she reminded herself, Jake was trained as an accountant to measure evidence and sift facts. Focusing on the things he knew, rather than the things he felt, allowed him to remain in control of an impossible situation.

She took a deep breath, and tried to follow Jake's example. But the first fact that came to her mind offered little comfort. "They've got a more powerful engine than we do," she said. "They're gaining on us." One glance over her shoulder proved the SUV was quickly closing the gap. Sunlight glinted off the windshield, making it impossible to see who was behind the wheel. Somehow, that made the situation more menacing, even though she doubted she'd recognize one of her father's many "associates." When she was growing up, they had been a series of faceless, muscular men who accompanied her father everywhere; they'd meant nothing to her.

The Subaru lurched as the back wheels skidded on the gravel shoulder. Anne shrieked, and clutched the dashboard with one hand, the fingers of her other hand digging into the armrest. "Slow down!" she pleaded. "We're going to run off the road."

He eased off on the gas pedal a little—enough that she felt she could breathe again. "We can't outrun them," he said. "So I'm going to slow down and see what they do."

"You're going to let them catch up with us?"

"They won't expect us to stop trying to outrun them. I'm hoping to catch them off guard."

"All right." She had to trust his judgment on this; she had no one else to turn to.

He eased off the gas and the Subaru slowed to forty, then thirty miles an hour. Anne watched in the side mirror as the SUV raced toward them, closing the gap between the two cars in an alarmingly short time. "They're going to ram us!" she screamed.

"No, they're not." He wrenched the steering wheel to the left, sending the Subaru shooting into the next lane, which was thankfully empty of oncoming traffic. The SUV flew past, a blur of black paint and red taillights.

Jake turned the wheel hard right, ramming the front end of the Subaru into the left rear quarter panel of the SUV. The SUV slid onto the gravel shoulder, sending up a rooster tail of mud and rock. The Subaru fishtailed wildly; Jake leaned forward, struggling to maintain control. "Hang on!" he shouted.

The car veered wildly to the left, narrowly avoiding a collision with the rock wall. The SUV slid along the right shoulder, only one wheel still in contact with the pavement. Anne watched in horror as the bulky black vehicle swayed, then began to topple, momentum taking it over the side. Time seemed to slow as the SUV plummeted, sending up sparks as it struck rock, bounced up, then tumbled out of sight.

Jake pulled the Subaru to the shoulder of the road and set the parking brake, but left the engine running. "Stay in the car," he ordered, and opened the driver's door.

She ignored the command, and followed him out of the car. On shaking legs, she walked along the shoulder of the road to the place where the SUV had gone over. Black skid marks cut into the gravel; a mirror torn from the side of the car rested on the rocks a few feet below. Trees blocked their view of the wrecked vehicle, but a plume of smoke marked the site of the crash. "Should we call for help?" she asked. "Do you think anyone is alive?"

"We'll call at the first place we come to with a phone," he said. "Meanwhile, we'd better get out of here."

She hugged her arms tightly across her stomach, fighting a chill that had nothing to do with the air temperature. "We can't just leave, can we?"

His eyes met hers, his gaze hard. "Do you want to answer a bunch of questions for the police?"

Questions that had no right answer, starting with "Who are you?" and "What are you doing with this man?"

She shook her head. "No, I don't want to get involved with the police."

"Come on, then." He took her elbow and led her back to the Subaru.

He didn't say anything for several minutes after they drove away, and she could find no words. Finally, as they neared a scenic overlook outside of Telluride, he pulled in and shut off the engine. "Are you okay?" he asked.

She laced her fingers together in her lap, as if she might squeeze all her turbulent emotions into a ball in the palms of her hands and keep them confined there, with no danger of them rocketing out of control or overwhelming her. "I think it's all just beginning to hit me," she said. "The man you killed at my house in Rogers—

DiCello—I remember him at my sixteenth birthday party. He wished me happy birthday. I'd forgotten all about that, and it came back to me this morning. And now he's dead."

"Because he tried to kill you."

"Yes, but…" She swallowed hard. "I don't think anyone is ever prepared for the idea that someone else—especially a parent—wants you to die. It's too bizarre."

"So is starting life over with a new name and a new story, trying to pretend the person you were never existed."

"I thought I was getting used to that." She stared out the window at the view of snow-capped mountains against a cobalt sky. So different from the jutting spires of city skyscrapers that had formed the backdrop of her old life. "When you go into witness protection, they give you a little training," she continued. "The counselors tell you to think of your new life as just that—a rebirth, a new beginning. They want you to focus on the positives and all the new possibilities, and not what you left behind. I thought I was handling it pretty well, until you came along."

"Because I brought all the memories of your old life back?"

"Because you brought back the memories of what happened at the end—why I had to hide in the first place." She studied his face, and curled her hands into fists to keep from reaching out and touching him, to reassure herself that he was indeed flesh and blood, and not a hallucination of her fevered imagination.

"I thought about you every day while I was in the hospital, and during rehab." He spoke low, the roughness in his voice catching at something in her chest and pulling. "I tried to get my friends at the Bureau to tell me where you were, but all I could get out of them was that you were safe. When I was well enough to be on my own, I started looking. I found the obituary for Elizabeth and figured out you must be in WitSec. It took a few more months of digging to find you after that—and only because I knew exactly what to look for."

"Was it awful—after the shooting? You haven't talked much about your injuries."

"It's not the most fascinating subject. I had some liver damage, shattered bones in my legs, pneumonia from a bullet in my lung. It took a lot longer to get back on my feet than I'd have liked, but I was motivated. And I was lucky. I trained for triathlons before I went undercover, so I was in good physical shape."

"I thought you were dead. Knowing my father had killed you was the final straw—the thing that turned me against him."

"I did die, in a way. Jake West died. Agent Westmoreland died. I had to learn to walk again, but I also had to learn to live a different kind of life. A life without you."

She tried to look away, but he reached up to brush her cheek, and gently turned her to face him once more. She raised her eyes to meet his; he was the same man she'd once loved so passionately, and yet he was not the same. In his eyes she saw a pain that touched her, and a new hardness that made her tremble.

He kissed her, his lips silencing her gasp. She closed her eyes and he deepened the kiss, his hand cradling her cheek, the tenderness of that touch, even more than the caress of his lips, breaking down some barrier within her. She sighed and leaned toward him, craving the closeness that had been denied her so long. Eyes closed, lips pressed to his, she gave herself up to memories of the intimacy they'd shared, and love she'd been sure would last forever.

The wail of a siren ripped apart the early morning silence. She shuddered, and pushed him away. "This is wrong," she said.

"Because I lied to you about my real identity?" His face was still very close to hers, so close she could see the individual bristles of the stubble along his jaw, and the fine lines of tension that radiated from the corners of his eyes. "I don't see how I could have done anything differently."

"It's wrong because neither one of us is the person we used to be. We don't even know each other."

"I know you're still as brave and beautiful as you ever were. And you understand loss and sacrifice. Those are hard lessons to learn, but in the end they make you a stronger, and hopefully a more compassionate, person."

He made her sound so noble and virtuous, like a saint, not a woman. "We don't want the same things," she said. "You want revenge. I just want to be left alone."

"You'll never be left alone until your father is behind bars again."

"You can't know that."

"I can't know anything, except that someone— probably your father—wants us dead and I have to do what I can to stop it."

He leaned back against the driver's seat and she breathed a little easier, relieved to shift the subject away from impossible emotions. "I can't understand how they keep finding us," she said. "I thought DiCello recognized my picture from the Telluride paper. But how did someone follow us to the cabin—and then find us again on the road? It's as if they have someone telling them our every move."

His expression hardened. "Not someone. Some*thing*." He shoved open the car door and climbed out.

"What are you doing?" she asked, but he ignored her. She exited the car in time to see him lie on the grimy snow and slide under the car.

"I don't know why I didn't think of this before." He emerged from beneath the car and stood, holding up a black plastic box about the size of a deck of cards. A green light glowed at one end of the device.

"What is that?" she asked.

"It's a GPS tracking device. It allows the person who planted it to track your movements—or the movements of the car. DiCello must have planted it before he entered your house."

"But he was there to kill me."

"Yes, but he probably had orders to plant the tracking device as insurance—in case you managed to get away."

She stared at the small black object, feeling sick. "What do we do now? Destroy it?"

"If we destroy it, they'll know we're on to them. We need to think of something else."

"What?"

A second emergency vehicle raced by, siren blaring. "Someone must have seen the smoke from the accident and reported it," he said.

She drew hands into the sleeves of her sweatshirt and hugged her arms across her stomach. "We have to get rid of that thing."

"Yes. And I think I know the perfect place. Get back in the car."

She returned to the passenger seat and had scarcely fastened her seat belt before he turned the car around and headed back the way they'd come. "What are you doing?" she asked.

"You'll see."

As they neared the place where their pursuers had run off the road, they saw the flashing lights of emergency vehicles. Jake parked on the side of the road behind a Colorado Highway Patrol SUV. "Wait here," he said.

He got out and walked alongside the patrol vehicle. An officer approached. "Sir, you need to leave," he said.

"I just wondered if there was anything I could do to help." He craned his neck to see down into the canyon, a nosy tourist drawn to the excitement.

"No sir, we have everything under control."

"What happened?" Jake asked.

"A car went over the side. It happens. People drive too fast, or maybe he fell asleep. We don't know yet."

"That's too bad. I'll have to be more careful out there."

"You do that. Now if you'll please leave."

"Of course." He turned, and stumbled, bracing himself against the side of the patrol car. "Sorry," he said. "Must have tripped on a rock." He straightened, nodded to the officer and returned to the car, walking briskly. "Someone went over the side," he said to Anne. "Shows you how dangerous these roads can be."

She waited until he'd turned the car and headed back toward Telluride before she asked, "What did you do?"

"When I stumbled, I stuck the tracking device on the side of the patrol vehicle."

"Why did you do that?"

"Instead of tracking us, whoever is after us can track the cops for a while."

"You don't think we're putting the police in danger?"

"If your father sends someone else to follow you, that person will recognize a cop car from a long way off. But chances are the cops will discover the tracking device long before your dad's thugs show up. Until they do, it buys us time to get settled in Telluride."

"If my father is there, what then?"

"We make sure he's there, and contact the authorities."

So he didn't intend to go after her father himself. The knowledge flooded her with relief. "There's a reward for finding him, isn't there? Patrick mentioned it."

"Yes. But that's not why I'm doing this."

"I know. But I like thinking you'd have the money from the reward to live on after I'm gone."

"Right." He looked grim. "While you're teaching school or working as a secretary in your new life."

"Teaching was the best part about starting over. I loved my students—I loved making my own way, based on my own merits. That's something I never had to do as Elizabeth Giardino."

"Then I hope you get the chance to do that again."

"What will you do when this is over?" she asked.

"I don't know. I suppose it depends on how things turn out. Come on. We've got to find a place to stay and do some shopping. We'll play tourists for a few hours, anyway, and worry about your father later."

"What about Patrick? I promised to contact him today."

"You can call him from the hotel later. But you'll need to try to put him off for another day or two, to give us time to look for your father."

"Patrick isn't the easiest person to put off."

"Then wait to call him. Tonight, let's just try to relax, and worry about the rest tomorrow."

She nodded. She'd grown used to not thinking much about tomorrow. Knowing, as she did, how things could change in an instant, she'd spent the last year focusing on right now, today. Tomorrow was a luxury she almost felt she couldn't afford, but for a little while, maybe, she could pretend things were different. Maybe, with Jake by her side, she could even be Elizabeth, a woman without a worry in the world, with the man who loved her more than anyone ever could.

Chapter Ten

The kiss had been a mistake. Jake had known that the moment his lips touched Anne's. If he was going to pull this off—if he was going to find Sam Giardino and see him locked away for good—he couldn't afford to make mistakes. He couldn't let emotion or nostalgia or plain old lust interfere with the job he had to do.

He glanced at the woman walking beside him. Showered and freshly made up, dressed in a fake-fur-trimmed parka, designer jeans and knee-high boots they'd purchased at a thrift store on Telluride's main drag, Anne looked more like Elizabeth when he'd first met her—polished and fashionable and way out of his league.

"What are you staring at?" she asked.

"I'm not staring." He turned his attention back to the crowded street in front of them. Men and women filled the sidewalks and spilled out of shops and restaurants, talking and laughing, carrying shopping bags or schlepping skis and snowboards toward the gondola that would take them up to the ski resort above town. Conversations in four languages drifted to him, and he heard accents that identified the speakers as hailing from New York and Texas and half a dozen foreign countries. February was the height of the tourist season in Telluride, and somewhere in all this humanity was one man who'd managed to evade the law for the past year. Jake had to admire Giardino's cunning; a crowded tourist town with people from all over the world was the perfect place for a fugitive to hide, lost in a crowd of people who didn't know one another and would likely never see each other again.

Jake and Anne had arrived in town a little after ten in the morning and found lodging at a new hotel that had been built to blend in with the town's Victorian architecture. He'd booked them into adjoining rooms and they'd agreed to meet later for lunch and shopping. The afternoon should have been a pleasant break from the tension, but the events of the past two days, and the real reason they were here, prevented them from completely relaxing and enjoying their roles as tourists. "I've been thinking about how we're going to find your father," he said.

"Yes. How are we going to do that?"

"If he's here to ski, we need to hit the slopes."

"Do you ski?" she asked.

"Not in a long time. What about you? Do you make it to Telluride much from Rogers?"

"I've been a few times. Enough to be fairly familiar with the runs."

"Good. Then you can take us to the places your father's likely to hang out."

"It's a big mountain, with a lot of people. I don't think our chances are very good that we'll see him."

"You say that because you don't really want to see him."

She stiffened, and started to protest; then she clamped

her mouth shut and shook her head. "No, I don't want to see him. Why should I?"

"Help me find him and you'll never have to see him again."

She took hold of his arm, stopping him. "Why is this so important to you? You're retired. You don't have to do this anymore."

"I told you—neither one of us will be safe as long as he's walking around free."

"This isn't about safety—it's about revenge. You want to make him pay because he hurt you."

"I want to make him pay because he hurt *you*."

She released his arm as if she'd been burned. "Don't make this about me. I was happy with my life the way it was."

This was all about her. If Jake hadn't fallen in love with her, if he hadn't let his emotions get the better of his training and common sense, he might not have been so careless and let himself be found out. He wouldn't have almost died in a hail of bullets and she wouldn't have been dragged away and persuaded to testify against her father. She wouldn't have had to hide out in WitSec and she wouldn't be running from her father's thugs right now. If he did nothing else with his life, he had to fix this mistake. He couldn't give her back the life she'd had, or even repair the damage to their own relationship. But he could see that she was safe. Then, even if he had to leave her—and he did have to leave her, she'd made that clear enough—he'd have done what he could to make up for the mistakes of the past.

"Fine. It's not about you," he said. "It's about me. I screwed up and I have to make this right. Your father belongs behind bars. It was my job to put him there and I want to finish the job."

"You don't work for the Bureau anymore."

"No, I don't. Which makes this both easier and more difficult."

She looked at him, head tilted slightly to one side, one eyebrow raised. He remembered that look from before, imperious and demanding answers. He almost smiled, seeing her so easily slip back into the role of the pampered princess who was used to getting her way. "Easier, because I don't have to wait and go through channels, or play by their rules," he explained. "Harder, because I have no authority, and I don't have the Bureau's resources at my fingertips, or a team backing me up."

"Only me." She looked away before he could judge the expression in her eyes. "Do you think finding my father will prove they were wrong to dismiss you?" she asked. "Do you think it will get your job back?"

"This isn't about getting my job back." He wasn't a good fit for the Bureau; he was always stepping outside the boundaries of his job description and questioning dictates from higher up the chain of command. Going to Sam Giardino's warehouse hadn't been part of his job. He was an accountant, and he was supposed to stay chained to his desk in front of a computer. But his bosses had badly wanted the dirt on the Giardino family, and when they'd learned Jacob had an in, they had been willing to overlook him breaking the rules. Only when his rule-breaking had resulted in a disaster had they been more than happy to let him go. "Though I would have preferred to leave on my own terms, not theirs," he said. And yes, it would feel good to prove to them they had been wrong to dismiss him so easily.

"You said something before about my father escaping prison with the help of a politician. Do you mean the governor?"

"I don't know who. I couldn't find anyone who would admit to being part of the investigation, only that there is an investigation. Someone with power pulled strings so that your father got what he needed to get out of prison. Two guards died during the escape, did you know that?"

"Yes. I know my father is a murderer." Her expression grew bleak. "I've known it for a very long time, but I either ignored the killings or tried to tell myself they were justified. You opened my eyes to the truth of what he'd done, and when he tried to kill you…"

He put his arm around her. "I read the trial transcripts. Your testimony was the key to convicting your father. I know speaking out against him wasn't an easy thing to do."

"It wasn't as hard as you might think. I was so angry. I wanted to hurt him."

"And now?"

"Now I'm more sad than angry. And tired." She stifled a yawn.

He patted her shoulder and released her. "You must be dead on your feet. We've both hardly slept."

"I'm too keyed up to sleep." She shrugged away from him. "Maybe we could get something to eat."

At the mention of food, his stomach growled. He couldn't remember his last real meal. "There are plenty of places to choose from. See anything you like?"

"There was a little bistro a few blocks back. Let's try that."

They retraced their steps. The sun was sinking fast behind the mountains; with dusk came a deeper cold, and more crowds, as vacationers and locals alike returned from a day on the slopes. Jake kept one hand on Anne's back to prevent them from being separated, but also because he felt the need to hold on to her. Today he'd glimpsed the vulnerability beneath her strength. He wanted her to know she wasn't alone in this, that he'd do anything to protect her.

They'd almost reached the restaurant when Anne froze. Tension radiated from her body, like a hunting dog on point—or a rabbit that knew it had been spotted by a dog. Jake moved in close behind her. "What is it?" he asked softly.

"I thought I saw Sammy."

"Your brother?"

"Yes." She continued to stare in the direction of the brewpub across the street. "He just went into that restaurant. I'm sure it was Sammy. He's here in Telluride."

ANNE HADN'T SEEN her brother since the trial, but it wasn't as if he would have changed that much in a year. "Are you sure it was him?" Jake asked.

"Yes." She'd scarcely glimpsed the dark-haired man who'd entered the restaurant with two burly companions, but something in the set of his shoulders and the back of his head had sparked instant recognition. Her heart had leapt in her chest, blood calling to blood.

"Did he see you?" Jake asked.

"No."

"Then we'd better not give him the chance." He took

her arm and led her away. She went reluctantly, finding it difficult to move, when all she wanted to do was run toward her brother. She wanted to feel his arms around her and hear him tell her he was glad to see her—that everything would be all right.

She shook her head, as if she could shake out that fantasy. It had been a while since she and Sammy had been really close; he was four years younger and involved in his own life. As the only son he'd been groomed to follow in her father's footsteps. While she'd been spoiled and pampered and indulged, Sammy had endured lectures and ordeals designed to toughen him up and teach him the ins and outs of the various family "businesses."

They turned onto the next block. Jake stopped in the shelter of an overhang in front of a boutique and let the crowd flow around them. "I don't think we were followed," he said.

"I'm sure he didn't see me."

"If your brother is here, that means your father is probably here, too," Jake said.

"Maybe. Or he could have come here on vacation with his family." His family and a few spare goons to act as bodyguards and lookouts. The thought made her stomach churn.

"I didn't see too much of Sammy while I was with your family. He was away a lot."

"My father had sent him to Atlantic City to learn about the Giardino operation there."

"Were you close?"

"We were when we were younger. I always looked out for him." She smiled, remembering the nights she'd sneaked into Sammy's room with a peanut butter sandwich when he'd been sent to bed without his supper, or the times she'd finished his homework assignments for him. "We were the only kids around most of the time," she said. "So the two of us would band together to spy on the adults. But as we got older, we kind of grew apart." Her smile faded. "It's hard to be close in a family where there are so many secrets and lies."

He put his hand on her shoulder, a comforting gesture. She fought the urge to lean into him. She was physically and emotionally exhausted, not just from the events of the last few days, but from months of bearing everything alone. WitSec had helped her start over with a new life, but it couldn't erase the memories of everything that had happened. Figuring out what to do with those memories, how to process and deal with them while not letting them destroy her, was wearing.

"I'm going to ask you a question you may not like, but I want you to answer honestly," he said. "Your brother is next in line to assume power. Do you think he'd order a hit on you?"

"If you mean is he the one behind everything that's been happening lately, I don't know." She met his gaze and saw her own exhaustion and frustration reflected in her eyes. "Since Sammy is the only son, he was always more involved in the business side of things than I was. I saw more of his wife those last few years than I did him, so I have no idea what he thinks of me these days. I never would have believed my father wanted me dead, and he actually threatened me. I can't wrap my mind around my brother feeling that way about me."

"I don't recall that you and his wife were that close. Stacy—that was her name, right?"

"Yes. I liked her well enough, but she never really fit

in well with the rest of the family." Stacy was neither brash and outspoken, nor meek and compliant, the two models for Giardino women. She held herself aloof, and maintained a slightly disapproving air. "I didn't understand her at the time, but now that I'm on the outside, I have more sympathy." Barely nineteen when she'd married Sammy Giardino, Stacy Franklin had been thrust into a world where she didn't fit. She must have felt trapped in her contentious marriage; divorce was not an option in the Giardino family, since ex-spouses had the potential to reveal family secrets.

"I got the impression she wasn't very happy in her marriage," Jake said.

"Probably not. It was more a political move on my father's part than a love match."

"You mean your father arranged the marriage? And Sammy went along?"

"Sammy will do anything to please my father." Even though Sam Senior was almost impossible to please.

"Maybe he resents the control your father has over his life."

"Maybe."

"Then maybe we can use that. Maybe he'll help us get to your father."

"I doubt that. I mean, he might want to get back at my father, but doing so would mean destroying everything Sammy is supposed to inherit—everything he's spent his life working toward. I can't see him giving up all that."

"If I could arrange for you to talk to him, would you?"

"I don't know. Yes. But because I want to see him, not because I think it will be of any help." To spend even a few minutes with someone who knew her—knew her childhood and her relatives, with whom she had shared so many memories and experiences—would be such a gift. Of all the things she'd experienced since going into witness protection, the loneliness of having no family at all had been the most unexpected pain.

She became aware of Jake studying her intently, as if trying to read her mind. "Are you all right?" he asked.

"I don't feel like braving a restaurant right now," she said. "Let's go back to the hotel and order room service."

"All right."

They didn't speak as they walked back to their hotel, though Jake radiated tension. He scanned the crowd, watching for her brother or father, she supposed. She couldn't help watching, too, but saw no one familiar in the sea of strangers' faces.

At the hotel, he followed her into her room and checked the bathroom and closet. "Do you really think someone is hiding out here, waiting to pounce?" she asked when he returned from the bathroom.

"Probably not. But better to be safe." He picked a room service menu from the dresser. "What do you want to eat?"

"Some soup. I don't care what kind."

He called in the order, then settled into the room's one chair, while she sat on the side of the bed. "All right if I eat in here with you?" he asked.

She shrugged. She didn't want to be alone, but she didn't want him hovering, either. "I should call Patrick," she said.

"And tell him what?"

"Whatever I want," she snapped. She picked up the

receiver from the phone by the bed. "If I don't call, he'll think something's wrong." But of course, a lot of things were wrong. Someone—probably her father—was trying to kill her. A man she thought was dead had come back to life. She'd seen her brother for the first time in a year, and part of her had been afraid to let him see her. Nothing in her life was as it ought to be.

She dialed his number. One of her first assignments as an enrollee in Witness Security had been to memorize the number.

He answered on the second ring. "Hello?"

"Hi. It's Anne. I wanted to let you know I'm all right."

"Where are you? What have you been doing? Why haven't you been answering your phone?" The rapid-fire questions betrayed his agitation, though his voice remained calm.

"I don't have my phone anymore. I, uh, I lost it." She doubted he would believe the lie, but she felt compelled to try it. She didn't want to alarm him, to make him want to rush her back into WitSec. She wasn't ready yet to change her name and her job and her life all over again. Not when she had a chance to stop her father—and to make things right with Jake.

"Where are you now?"

She hesitated. Lying to this man who'd been her only real friend this past year was impossible. "I'm in Telluride. At a hotel."

"Are you alone?"

She glanced toward Jake and found him watching her, eyes burning. "Jake is with me," she said.

"Are you all right? Has he tried to hurt you?"

"No! I mean, I'm fine. Jake has asked me to help

him find my father." Jake was shaking his head, but she turned away from him.

"He has no business contacting you." Patrick sounded angry. "And he has no business with your father. He's not a federal agent and he could be charged with interfering with an ongoing investigation. He's putting you in danger."

She had put herself in danger by agreeing to come with him. "Patrick, listen," she said. "I think my father might be here—in Telluride."

"What makes you think that? Have you see him?"

"No. But today I thought I saw my brother, Sammy. And the man who attacked me at my house in Rogers had a Telluride lift ticket on his jacket."

"Then you shouldn't be there. I want you to leave town immediately. Go back to the cabin where you were staying. You said that was safe, right?"

"Someone set fire to the cabin last night," she said. "Or rather, very early this morning, while we were asleep. We got away, but then they tried to run us off the road. Jake found a tracking device on my car. He thinks the man who came to my house in Rogers planted it."

Jake stood and made a move as if to grab the phone, but she leaned out of his way. "I really think we're close," she told Patrick. "As soon as we've located my father, I'll call and tell you. You can send federal agents in to make the arrest."

"I should come now, and get you away from there," Patrick said. "We can take it from here."

"If you send a bunch of feds into town, my father is going to find out," she said. "Let Jake and me see what we can find out first. We'll be careful."

"This isn't your fight anymore."

"I'm sorry, Patrick, but it is. He's my father and he's trying to kill me. I have to see for myself that he can't harm me anymore. That's the only way I can get on with my life."

"Letting you stay goes against everything I've pledged to do."

"If you come to town now and interfere with this, I'll leave and you'll never hear from me again."

"Don't do that."

"Then don't force my hand."

Silence. She could almost hear him thinking. Jake stood beside her, hands on his hips, glaring down at her. "I'll compromise," Patrick said. "I'll station a team near there, and when you give the word we'll move in. If you need anything in the meantime, call me. And don't do anything foolish. And don't let Jake do anything foolish."

"I won't."

"Be careful around him, Anne. He's not the man you knew before. Word is he's been obsessed with this case. Obsessive people don't act rationally."

What was rational about any of this? But she didn't bother pointing that out to Patrick. "I'll be careful," she said. "And I'll stay in touch."

"I'll only give you a few days. Then I will find you."

"A few days is all I'm asking. My father is either here or he isn't. We should know soon."

She hung up the phone. "What did he say?" Jake asked.

"He's going to station a team nearby, but he won't make any move until I tell him."

"Do you believe him?"

"I do. They want to find my father as badly as you do."

"Did you mean that—about leaving if they interfered?"

"Yes." She met his gaze, resolve strengthening in her. "I've run away from my father long enough. I need to end this once and for all."

Chapter Eleven

The next morning Anne and Jake dressed in the ski clothes they'd also purchased at the thrift shop, and rode the gondola up the mountain to the ski resort, where they rented equipment and purchased lift tickets. "What now?" Anne asked, when she'd followed Jake up the stairs to the base of the first ski lift.

"Now we wait. We hang out here, watch people coming off the gondola and boarding the lift, see if you spot anyone familiar."

She looked around at the skiers and snowboarders who stood in groups on the cobblestones of the ski village or queued up to board the lift. Dressed in helmets or knitted caps and brightly colored jackets and pants, they looked like circus performers, or aliens. "How am I going to recognize anyone when they're dressed like this?" she asked.

"You'll recognize your father or your brother."

"Will I?" Maybe she'd been wrong about seeing Sammy yesterday. After all, she'd only glimpsed him for a second. Maybe her imagination had played tricks on her.

"You will." Jake patted her shoulder. "Your subconscious will, even if your conscious self doubts."

"Is that the kind of thing they teach you at the Bureau?"

"No. I read it in a book somewhere."

"Don't believe everything you read."

She started to move toward the lift, but he stopped her. "We can see more hanging out down here than we can actually skiing."

"I think we can see a lot from the lift."

"No. This is where the action is."

Reluctantly, she slotted her skis alongside his in a rack and found a chair outside the bar and restaurant at the base of the lift that transported skiers up the mountain. "If this is all we were going to do, we could have worn our street clothes," she grumbled. "We could have told anyone who asked that we were waiting for our children to get out of ski school."

"Really? How many children? Boy or girl? Or maybe one of each."

She glared at him.

"If things had worked out differently we might have a child by now," he mused. "Though he—or she—would be too young to learn to ski."

Pain squeezed her heart as she thought of the baby she and Jake might have had. First, there would have been a huge society wedding, maybe at St. Patrick's Cathedral. Her father would have spared no expense for his only daughter. She'd have had a designer gown and a diamond tiara and a reception that people would have talked about for months afterward.

She and her new husband would have settled into a condo her father owned, and her husband would work in the family business, while she stayed home and raised children. On Sundays, they'd dine with her parents and her brother and his family, and there'd be no such thing as a holiday alone.

It was an old-fashioned lifestyle, one in which the women didn't work or have any independence of their own, so the reality would have been much less comfortable than the fantasy, but it had been her dream, until Jake had showed her the cruelty and ugliness beneath that pretty picture of family devotion. Once he'd opened her eyes, the dream hadn't seemed so lovely.

"Pay attention." Jake tapped the back of her hand. "Do you see anyone in the lift line or skiing down the mountain that you recognize?"

She scanned the crowd. "No."

"I think I'd recognize your father," Jake said. "I didn't see Sammy enough to be sure of recognizing him. But I'm guessing anyone who's skiing with a couple of burly bodyguards will stand out."

"You might be surprised," she said. "A lot of celebrities ski here. Some of them probably have bodyguards."

"I don't think even I would confuse your dad and some pop star."

Would a year on the run have aged her father? Or would time spent apart make her see him differently? "I don't think sitting here waiting is going to do us much good," she said. "From the lift we can see more."

"Fine. You go ski. I'm staying here."

She stood. "You can't ski, can you? You lied to me."

"I can ski. Or I could, before last year."

The image of him lying in a pool of blood on the floor of that hotel ballroom flashed into her mind and she felt sick. "I'm sorry. Your legs were injured. I didn't think—"

He waved away her apology. "I could probably still do it if I had to, but I'll be more mobile here. You go on and if you see anything, call me."

"All right." She should be safe enough by herself with people all around, and she had her phone to summon help. She put on her skis and moved into the line for the lift. This wasn't her first visit to Telluride; she'd come last year with a group of teachers and spent the day exploring the slopes. It had been one of her best days since coming to Rogers—one of the days when she hadn't felt so alone.

She rode up the lift with a mother, father and daughter from Texas. The ski runs spread out below the lift like a white carpet, skiers and snowboarders zipping along like toys on a track.

Her father would have moved away from the main ski area as quickly as possible. He didn't like crowds or waiting in line. The lifts farther from the base area would be less crowded, the terrain more challenging. She thought back to her previous visit to the resort, and other ski vacations she'd taken with her family. What runs would most appeal to her father?

At the top of the lift, she skied to a map of the area and studied it. Her father liked to show off. He liked to prove to himself, and to the men around him that, though he was getting older, he was still a man to be feared. He didn't, as he'd said on one of those long-ago vacations, want to ski with a bunch of women and children.

Anne decided he'd head for a group of double black diamond runs that hurtled down narrow, tree-lined slopes into territory that had been backcountry skiing until only a few years before. She'd make her way over to Revolution Bowl. There would be fewer skiers there; if her father was among them, she'd be sure to spot him.

As she skied to the next lift, she began to relax a little. The snow was smooth and perfect, the sun bright and the temperature not too cold. She was a strong skier, and she was safe here. No one was likely to recognize her in her secondhand ski clothes, her hair stuffed under a rented helmet. She was an anonymous tourist, free to move around as she chose.

She rode a second lift farther up the mountain and made her way to yet another lift that took her to the top of Revolution Bowl. From the top, she had a view of the entire resort and the town below. Half a dozen other skiers joined her at the start of the group of runs, none of them her father. Only one other woman was there— she smiled and nodded to Anne, who returned the nod.

Maybe she'd been wrong. Maybe now that her father was older, he no longer attempted such challenging terrain.

She pointed her skis down the slope and started down the run, her heart in her throat. It was steeper than she'd anticipated. The group she'd been with last year hadn't ventured into this terrain, labeled *expert only* on the map. Trees formed a dark green wall on either side of the narrow chute, forcing her to make tight turns. So much for her brilliant ideas. It was going to take all she had in her to get down from here onto more manageable terrain.

She stopped to rest at the side of the run and looked back up at the section she'd just skied. Probably a mistake, since it was steeper than anything she remem-

bered skiing before. But she told herself if she'd come
this far, she'd be fine....

Something about the stance of the skier coming
down the mountain toward her made her breath catch.
She shrank farther into the shelter of the trees and stared
as the man moved nearer, trailed by a burlier man. The
first skier wore black pants and a dark blue jacket, while
his companion was dressed all in black. He descended
the run in a series of sharp, aggressive turns, attacking
the snow as if determined to subdue it.

Her first thought was that she was watching her father, but as the man skied closer, she thought it must
be Sammy. He was broader across the shoulders than
her father, younger and more athletic. She prayed he
wouldn't notice her, hiding here in the trees.

In horror, she watched as he skied to a stop directly
in front of her. "Hello," he said. "We don't see many
women over on this side of the mountain."

She angled herself away, and pulled her fleece neck
gaiter over her nose and mouth. *"Excusez-moi, je ne
parle pas anglais,"* she said, in a high, breathy voice
that was partly an act and partly due to the fact that she
was having trouble breathing.

"I might have known, a European," he said to his
bodyguard, who'd stopped slightly behind him. He
turned back to Anne, and in perfect French, said. "I
usually ski in Europe myself, but decided to try here
this year. Are you enjoying the runs?"

Idiot. She'd forgotten Sammy had studied with the
same French tutor she had. Her father had seen knowing French as a sign of sophistication, and useful when
the family traveled to Europe. "I really must join my

husband now," she said, still in French, and started to move away.

Sammy's grip on her arm was firm, but not too rough. "Don't run off so soon," he said. "Did your husband leave you up here alone? That wasn't very gentlemanly. You should stick with me and we'll make him jealous."

She stifled a groan. She'd forgotten that her brother was an incorrigible flirt. He was convinced no woman could resist him—and many of them didn't. Though he wasn't the handsomest of men, money and power were an amazing aphrodisiac.

"That really would not be a good idea, monsieur," she said, and shot past him.

"Well, if you want to play it that way," he called, and took off after her.

On the edge of panic, Anne hurtled down the narrow, steep chute, skiing faster and more recklessly than she ever had. Why had she ever come up here? She should have listened to Jake, and stayed safely at the bottom of the mountain. No telling what Sammy would do if he found out his flirt was instead his sister—that is, if she even survived this perilous descent.

She shot out of the trees, into the open bowl. If she hadn't been so frightened, she might have enjoyed the treeless, more moderate terrain. But her only thought now was to get away from Sammy and lose herself in the crowd.

She glanced over her shoulder and saw that he was still close behind her. "Wait!" he shouted. "I only want to talk to you."

She took off, sure she would get away now. He was red-faced and out of breath, heavier and more out of shape than she was. She was skiing well, gaining confidence, and she began to relax, energized by her narrow escape. Wait until she told Jake about this…

Suddenly, she was falling. Her ski caught an edge and she faltered and was thrown to the ground, landing in a heap in soft snow, unhurt, but stopped.

As she struggled to her feet, Sammy skied up beside her. "Are you all right?" he asked, sticking to French.

She nodded, careful to keep her head down, her eyes focused on finding one ski that had detached in the fall and clicking back into it.

"You don't have to be afraid of me, you know," Sammy said. "I'm a good guy. Isn't that right, Carl?"

Carl, a looming hulk on Sammy's right, nodded. "Of course."

Anne said nothing, having decided that silence was the best option. Maybe he'd mistake her terror for shyness, or even a European disdain for the pushy American.

"You look so familiar," Sammy continued. "I'm sure we've met before. Where are you from? Paris? Or maybe Nice?"

She shook her head, and skied away. There was nothing he could do here on the slopes, she'd decided. He could follow her and he could talk to her, but he wouldn't grab her or force her to reveal her face. He still saw her as a possible romantic interest. With any luck, he'd give up before they reached the bottom of the mountain.

"Seriously, I'm sure I know you," he called, and raced after her.

He skied so close she was afraid he was going to cause a collision. Maybe that was what he wanted—

another fall he could help her up from, maybe while pulling the gaiter from her face and seeing her more clearly.

She pushed on, skiing faster. Recklessly. Her legs were shaky with fatigue, and her pounding heart wasn't helping matters any. If only there was some way to get rid of him.

She managed to put a little distance between them, but Sammy was determined and she had no doubt he'd catch up to her soon. She looked around for some escape—a run she could dart onto, or other people who might intervene.

Her rescue came from the most unlikely quarter. Hurtling toward them in an awkward half-crouch came a figure dressed in bright orange pants and a blue jacket—the clothing Jake had chosen at the thrift store yesterday.

Chapter Twelve

As Jake neared Sammy and Carl, he straightened and began windmilling his arms—the picture of an out-of-control skier. He slammed into the two men with a sickening thud. Anne winced, but couldn't look away. Sammy and Carl went sprawling into the snow, while Jake slid off to the side, skis still on his feet as he crouched over them.

She watched in amazement as he straightened, then skied past her without a word. She took off after him. By the time Sammy and Carl recovered, she and Jake would be long gone.

She followed him onto a series of blue and green runs that crisscrossed through the trees. He left the run and skied into the trees, stopping at the base of a large pine. He was breathing heavily, his face flushed when he pulled the bandana he wore from over his nose. "I think…we lost them," he gasped, doubled over, his hands on his knees.

She looked back up the run they'd just descended. No sign of her brother or his bodyguard. "What were you doing up there?" she asked. "I thought you were going to wait at the base."

"After you got on the lift I decided it was a bad idea

to leave you alone. If your father or one of his men recognized you, it would be too easy for them to kidnap you—or worse—without me to watch your back. So I followed."

"And I'm glad you did. But I thought you couldn't ski with your injuries."

"After that run I don't have much more left in me. I thought I was going to have to take off my skis and come down on my butt. Then I saw you with those two and adrenaline kicked in. Was that your brother?"

She nodded. "He didn't recognize me. I pretended to be a French tourist."

"And he believed you?"

"Oh, yes. My brother fancies himself a real Casanova, a man no woman can resist."

"You mean, he was *hitting* on you?" Jake's outrage was almost comical.

"Yes. It's funny now, but at the time, I was terrified." She looked him up and down. "Are you sure you're all right? That was quite a crash."

"I was a lot more stable than I looked, and I wasn't going that fast when I hit. Mainly, I surprised them and caught them off balance."

"I don't think they were hurt, either, but it bought us the time we needed to get away." She looked again up the empty run. "Do you speak French?"

He shook his head. "Why?"

"I was thinking that if we run into them again before we get off this mountain—if they see us together—you need to pretend to be my husband. I told them I was trying to get back to you."

"Tell them I have laryngitis."

She laughed, as much from relief as from any real

mirth. "I'm so glad you came along when you did," she said. "I was sure any moment he'd recognize me. He'd be embarrassed and angry, and there's no telling what he would have done. Or rather, what he would have had Carl do."

"At least now we know for sure he's here. I don't suppose he said anything about your father?"

"No. And I certainly wasn't going to ask."

"We'd better go. We'll head back through the beginner area. Something tells me your brother and his bodyguard aren't likely to venture onto the bunny hill."

"I think the bunny hill is all I care to tackle right now," she said. "My legs are jelly."

"Mine, too. Just hang in there. We'll return to the hotel and decide on our next move."

"I vote for the hot tub," she said.

He grinned. "Sounds like a great idea."

He led the way out of the woods and she followed. Later, when the impact of her encounter with her brother really hit her, she'd probably be even more shaky. For now, she pushed those emotions away and focused on keeping her weight even over her skis and making nice, easy turns. She was safe, and Jake was watching her back. Amazing how good it felt to know that.

"ARE YOU SURE you're all right?" Jake asked for the third time since he and Anne had clicked out of their skis and headed back toward the hotel.

"I'm fine." She strode along beside him, skis on her shoulder, goggles shading her eyes—and hiding her expression, so he couldn't decide if she was telling the truth or putting up a brave front.

"Are you sure? You look pale."

"You're the one who's limping, not me."

He made an effort to lessen the limp, though his legs felt like they were made of broken glass, jagged edges sending jolts of pain through him with every step. "The physical therapist said exercise was good for me." Exercise, but probably not a kamikaze plunge down a double-black ski slope.

"I'm sure I could have gotten away from Sammy and his sidekick on my own," she said. "I hate to think you hurt yourself coming after me when it wasn't really necessary."

"A while ago you were grateful to me for saving you."

"Yes, but now I've had time to think about it and I realize I didn't really need saving. I could have kept up the pretense of being French and eventually gotten away from him. Once we'd been around more people, he wouldn't have wanted to make a scene."

Maybe Jake had risked himself for nothing; even when he'd known Anne before, she'd been very good at looking after herself. "If nothing else, you could have shown off your boxing skills and punched him," he said.

She laughed. "There is that."

"So what now?" he asked. "Back to the hotel and that hot tub?"

"First, I have to buy a swimsuit."

"Can you buy a swimsuit in a ski town?"

She smiled. "Of course."

She led the way down a side street to a boutique that, as it turned out, had a large section devoted to both men's and women's swimwear. They left their skis in a rack just outside the door and pushed their way inside. Shoppers, mostly women, milled around the racks and displays, while several men congregated on benches in what was clearly a waiting area for patient spouses.

Anne selected several suits and headed for the dressing room. "Need any help?" Jake asked.

"You need to get your own suit," she said, and ducked into a changing room.

He wandered over to a rack of Hawaiian-print swim trunks and began flipping through them. "You're taking a risk coming here, Senator," a voice behind him said.

"Even politicians are allowed to take vacations."

"The issue isn't your vacation. It's who you're vacationing with."

Jake maneuvered around the rack of suits until he had a view of the speakers—two middle-aged men seated on a bench near the door, apparently waiting for their wives or girlfriends to finish shopping.

"I'm vacationing with my wife and with you and your wife, Al," a portly, white-haired man with a florid face said. "Do you have a problem with that?"

"I'm not the one you should be worried about," the other man, shorter with iron-gray hair, said.

"This really isn't a discussion I want to have in public," the senator said.

"Should I get the red or the blue?" Jake turned to see Anne holding up two swimsuits for his inspection.

"No bikini?" he asked, surveying what looked to him like relatively demure one-pieces.

"I guess you'll have to use your imagination," she said.

"I have a very good imagination." And a good memory.

"Have you picked out a suit?" she asked.

"How about this one?" He grabbed a pair of trunks from the rack.

"You don't think they're a little big?"

He checked the tag. Extra large. He found the same pair in a medium. "Okay, how about these?"

"Great. What have you been doing while I've been in the dressing room? Ogling other women?"

"Not exactly." He pulled out his credit card to pay for their purchases, then steered her outside. When they were a block away from the shop, he asked, "Does your father know Senator Greg Nordley? He's a senator from New York state."

"I know who he is, but I have no idea if Pop knew him. Maybe. Probably. He made it a point to know people like that."

"People like what?"

"People in power. Politicians. Why?"

"I just saw a man I think is Nordley in that shop. He was talking to another man who apparently thought Nordley was taking a risk by vacationing in Telluride with someone the other guy didn't approve of."

"You think Nordley is here to see my father?"

"It makes sense if Nordley is the man who helped your father get out of prison. Maybe Nordley is here to collect a favor."

She said nothing as they negotiated a crowded corner. "Did your FBI contacts say the man who helped my father was a senator? Or that it was a politician from New York?"

"They didn't say. But it makes me wonder."

She looked doubtful. "It's not much to go on."

"Let's file the information away for future reference. It could come in handy."

"I don't see how, but all right." She shifted her skis to her other shoulder. "Right now all I want is a shower and a soak in that hot tub."

"Sounds good." He was looking forward to seeing her in her swimsuit, but he'd keep that comment to himself—for now.

AN HOUR LATER, Jake, wrapped in a hotel robe and carrying a towel, rode the elevator to the rooftop hot tub, where Anne had agreed to meet him after her shower.

The elevator opened and he stepped onto the deck, which offered an extravagant view of snowcapped peaks and azure sky. At this time of day, just after noon, the deck was empty, the large, bubbling hot tub awaiting the après-ski crowd later in the day.

He made his way to the spa, grateful Anne wasn't around to see him limping. That mad dash down the mountain had taken more out of him than he would admit to her. Only sheer will and obstinacy had gotten him through. Then again, that was what had been driving him ever since he opened his eyes in the hospital after the shooting—a will to survive and a determination to finish the job he'd started and see Sam Giardino behind bars permanently.

He carefully lowered himself into the steaming water and positioned himself to watch the elevator doors. He didn't want to miss a moment of Anne in her swimsuit. The modest one-piece she'd purchased was not the daring bikini Elizabeth would have chosen, but he had no doubt she'd be more beautiful than ever in it.

And he was going to do his best to not show his re-action to her. They had a business arrangement and a tentative friendship; he wouldn't do anything to jeopardize either.

The elevator doors opened and he sat up straighter, heart pounding in anticipation. But instead of Anne, a man stepped onto the deck. He was tall, with light brown hair showing beneath a red knit cap. He wore hiking boots, dark jeans and a fisherman's sweater. To most people, he probably looked like a tourist, but something in his alert attitude—a sense of coiled energy and vigilance—told Jake this guy was either law enforcement or a paid hit man.

Chapter Thirteen

Jake froze, and tried to keep his breathing steady and even. Had Sam Giardino discovered that Jake was alive and in Telluride, and sent someone to take him out? After killing Jake, would the assassin wait on the roof for Anne?

He glanced at his robe hanging on the back of a chair, just out of arm's reach. There was a gun in the pocket, but he'd likely be dead before he could reach it. Gripping the edge of the hot tub, he looked around for something else he could use as a weapon. In the meantime, he needed to remain calm and avoid overreacting.

The newcomer walked straight to the hot tub. "Jacob Westmoreland," he said in a smooth, deep voice that belonged on the evening news. "I'm Patrick Thompson. I thought the two of us should talk."

Thompson. Jake released his grip on the side of the tub and sat up straighter. He might have known the marshal would show up sooner rather than later. "Does Anne know you're here?" he asked.

"No. I wanted to talk to you first." The marshal's gaze swept over him, assessing, though his expression betrayed nothing about his opinion of Jake.

"You wanted to check me out."

"That's my job." He looked around the empty rooftop. "I'll wait for you over by those tables."

Jake debated refusing, or making Thompson wait until he'd finished his soak. But that would allow more time for Anne to arrive, and he'd just as soon get this over with before she showed up.

Thompson walked over to the tables and took a chair facing Jake. Conscious of the other man's eyes on him, Jake took his time climbing out of the spa, toweling off and shrugging into his robe. Then he joined the federal marshal at the table. A propane heater shaped like an oversize copper lamp bathed the table in warmth, and provided a low, dull roar to further mask their conversation from passersby—if there had been anyone to overhear.

"Can I see some ID?" Jake asked, choosing a chair with a view of the elevator.

Thompson produced a leather case and opened it. Jake studied the U.S. marshal's credentials and nodded. "What do you want to talk about?" As if the two of them had any shared interests other than Anne.

"You were out of line, getting in touch with Anne. And you're stepping way over the line, bringing her here."

"She's in WitSec. She's not your prisoner. She can see whoever she wants, and go where she wants."

"You're not a federal agent anymore. This is not your case, and by getting involved you're jeopardizing a federal investigation."

"No, I'm a private citizen. I can visit a friend if I want to."

Thompson's jaw tightened, the first sign that the guy could show emotion. "You had no right to compromise

Anne's identity. If someone who knew her before sees the two of you together, you could be putting her in danger."

"You let her think I was dead." All the time he'd been worrying and wondering and dreaming about her, she hadn't even known he was alive.

"We thought it was best," Thompson said. "She needed to start over, with no ties to the past."

"I'm doing my best to give her a future. One where she doesn't have to be looking over her shoulder every minute."

He expected Thompson to object to that. Fine. Jake was ready to have it out with the man who thought he had the right to dictate the life Anne would lead. Instead, the marshal leaned back in his chair and studied Jake, relaxed and thoughtful. "What makes you think you can find Sam Giardino when no one else has?" he asked.

"Maybe because I want him more than the rest of you do."

Thompson stiffened and Jake bit back a smile. He didn't like criticism, did he? "What do you mean?" Thompson asked.

"I mean that it's in some people's interests to keep Sam Giardino free—people in power who owe him favors."

"Who are you talking about?"

He glanced toward the elevator—no sign of Anne. "I don't know yet," he said. "But you must have heard the same rumors I did."

"That depends on what you've heard."

"All I heard was that an elected official who knew how to pull strings worked it so that Sam Giardino got away, and provided the means for Giardino to stay free. Someone in power made it his business to see that Giardino didn't spend much time behind bars."

"But you can't give me a name?"

"No." He sat back, debating whether to share the next bit of news—or non-news—with Thompson. He decided to let the man decide for himself if the information was valuable or not. "I saw Senator Greg Nordley in town today. He was arguing with another man who thought the senator was taking a risk in coming to Telluride."

"Who was this man?"

"I don't know. But I'd recognize him again if I saw him."

"Maybe he was worried the senator would hurt himself skiing."

"This other man objected to whoever the senator was vacationing with."

"Anything else?"

"No. The senator said this wasn't something they should be discussing in public."

Thompson took a notebook from his pocket and wrote something—maybe Nordley's name. Or his assessment that Jake was nuts. "A U.S. senator could be doing any number of things—ethical or unethical, legal or illegal—but that doesn't mean any of them have a connection to Sam Giardino."

"Yeah. Maybe it's just a coincidence. But if I've heard this rumor about Sam's powerful friend, I know you have, too. And if we find Sam, he could lead us to that person."

"We?"

"Do I look like a one-man SWAT team? When I

find him, I'll let you and whatever posse you want to bring do the rest."

Thompson fell silent. His gaze dropped to Jake's legs, visible beneath the hem of the hotel robe. The scars from the surgery that had put him back together were clearly visible, white, waxy lines against his skin. "You're something of a legend, did you know?" Thompson asked. "They say you died twice on the operating table, and almost bought it again when you had pneumonia."

Was Thompson trying to flatter him? Jake had heard the legend line before—when the Bureau showed him the door and handed him a pension.

"All the more reason for me to want Giardino, to make him pay for the hell he put me through."

"They also say you're too obsessed with Giardino—that you've made this fight personal."

"Who is they? And I just told you this fight *is* personal."

"You lose your objectivity, you lose all sense of caution."

"Did they teach you that in Marshal school?"

To his surprise, Thompson laughed. "You don't sound like any Bureau man I ever met."

"I never was a typical FBI guy. I was an accountant who thought it would be fun to play secret agent. I found out otherwise."

Thompson leaned forward, elbows on his knees. "You and I are on the same side," he said. "We both want to protect Anne."

"Are you in love with her?" Jake looked Thompson in the eye, trying to gauge the marshal's reaction to the question.

The other man never flinched. "I like Anne and I have a lot of respect for her, but no, I'm not in love with her."

Jake believed him. "Of course not. Because that would be unprofessional and possibly unethical, and all the things that are probably in a file with my name on it somewhere at the Bureau."

"I haven't seen that file, but I heard you were in love with her once. Are you still?"

Jake looked away. "The point is, she's not in love with me, so let's leave it at that."

Neither man said anything for a long moment, the hiss of the propane heater and the bubbling hot-tub jets filling the silence between them. Jake went back to watching the elevator, wondering what was taking Anne so long, yet, at the same time, hoping she'd put off her arrival a few moments longer.

Thompson blew out a breath and sat up straight once more. "If you find Sam—and I still think that's a big if—what will you do after we arrest him?"

"I don't know."

"You mean you didn't plan for the future?"

"All those times on death's door taught me not to think too far ahead."

"Why do you think Sam Giardino is in Telluride?"

Jake was tired of Thompson's questions, but he figured the guy wouldn't leave unless he thought he had all the answers. He turned to face the marshal once more. "He's probably not right in town, but he's somewhere near here. Anne tells me he has lots of friends with money. One of them probably has a house around here they're letting him use as a secure hideout."

"That doesn't mean he's here."

"His son, Sammy, is here."

"When we spoke on the phone, Anne mentioned she thought she saw him, but it wasn't a positive ID."

"She saw him again this morning."

"Is she sure it was him?"

"Yes. She talked to him. He didn't know it was her. She pretended to be a French tourist and he decided to flirt with her. She was having trouble shaking him."

This news clearly alarmed Thompson. "She needs to leave here right away. This isn't worth endangering her life."

"It's my life, Patrick. I appreciate your concern, but I'm not going to run away again."

Both men looked up and found Anne walking toward them. She wore one of the white hotel bathrobes cinched tightly around her waist, and brown Ugg boots, the combination seeming somehow chic on her.

Thompson stood. Jake was slower to rise to his feet, but if Thompson was going to be such a gentleman, he wouldn't be outdone, even if his stiffening limbs protested.

All her attention was focused on Thompson, however. "Patrick, what are you doing here? I thought we agreed you were going to wait for my call."

"My job is to look after you. That includes keeping track of where you are."

"How did you find me?" she asked.

"Telluride isn't that big of a town. I only had to contact a few hotels with your description before I found the right one. And if it's that simple for me to locate you, your enemies wouldn't have any difficulty locating you, either."

Jake wanted to punch the man for trying to scare

her, but he should have known Anne wouldn't frighten easily. "I'm fine. You didn't have to follow me here."

"I had to make sure Jake wasn't putting you in danger."

She looked at Jake, a half smile playing at the corners of her mouth. "And what did you decide?"

"He told me you saw your brother today. That you talked to him. That's getting much too close."

"Sammy didn't recognize me."

"You were lucky this time. What if next time your luck has run out?" He fixed his dark gaze on her. "I know it's difficult to see family—people you love—as a danger to you. But you know your father is ruthless. He would kill you, if given the chance, even if you don't want to believe it."

"I don't want to believe it," she admitted. "But I know you're right. Which is why it's so important to lock him up again, where he can't get to me."

Jake realized she was repeating his words. Did she believe them now, or was she using them as a convenient way to put off Thompson?

"Now that we suspect he's in the area, you can leave," Thompson said. "We'll take it from here."

"How are you going to find him? My father hasn't avoided jail time all these years by not being able to spot law enforcement a mile away."

"He didn't spot Jake."

She flushed. "Jake isn't a typical agent, I don't think."

The frown lines on Thompson's forehead deepened. "I don't like it."

"But it's my decision to make," she said. "And I want to stay here and see if we can find my father. When we do, I promise I'll let you handle it."

Thompson looked at Jake. "Do you really trust him?"

"He hasn't given me any reason not to so far," she said.

"That isn't an answer."

"Then, yes. Yes, I trust him."

Jake moved to Anne's side. "Give us another couple of days to see if we can locate the Giardino hideout," he said. "We'll keep you informed, but give us room to work."

Thompson looked grim. "All right. I'll give you two days." He turned to Anne. "But at the first sign of trouble, call me. We're already working on a new plan for you, someplace where you'll be safe."

She nodded, though her eyes looked bleak. Jake wouldn't blame her if she balked at starting over yet again, with another new name, new job and new identity. How often could a person do that before she didn't know who she was anymore?

Thompson left them. When the elevator doors closed behind him, Jake said, "Let's get in the hot tub. We can talk there."

He lowered himself into the water quickly, submerging his legs before she got a good look at the scars. He wasn't a vain man, but he didn't want her feeling sorry for him, or thinking he was a freak. She took her time pulling off her boots, then slipped out of the robe and folded it neatly across the bench beside the hot tub.

His heart stopped beating for a few breaths, or at least it felt that way as he stared at her, at the blue Lycra swimsuit hugging the swell of her breasts, at the indentation of her waist and the flare of her hips. Her long, bare legs seemed perfect, and looking at them made him feel even more glad to be alive. As long as he lived, she would always be the standard by which he'd judge other women; time and the differences between them hadn't changed that. The beauty he saw in her wasn't merely a matter of physical appearance, though she'd always been a woman who turned heads wherever she went. He knew the loveliness of the woman she was inside—the intelligence and compassion and bravery that made her, to him, the most gorgeous person in the world.

"You can put your eyes back in your head now," she said as she slipped into the water across from him.

"Can't blame a guy for looking," he said. Too bad looking was all he'd do. Once she had welcomed his touch, but that seemed a long time ago. Despite the way she'd warmed to him over the last twenty-four hours, and her response to the one kiss they'd shared in the car, she'd made it clear that she didn't think the man she loved existed anymore—and the real man who'd showed up to take his place didn't measure up.

"Mmmmm." She sank lower in the water and closed her eyes. "So now that we've convinced Patrick that we can track down my father, how are we going to do it?"

"You could talk to Sammy. Arrange to meet him in some neutral location and see if you can persuade him it's to his benefit to turn the old man in."

"I don't think it would work."

"Because Sammy is more loyal to his father than you were?"

"He married Stacy to please my father."

"One more reason to resent the old man." Jake drummed his fingers on the side of the tub. "I wasn't a part of your household long, but from what I saw, your father rode Sammy pretty hard. He wasn't spoiled like you."

She opened her eyes. "That's because I was a woman—my father didn't expect anything from me. He was hard on Sammy because he thought that was the way to make him hard, to prepare him to be the boss one day."

"Maybe so. But that kind of treatment gets old, especially now that Sammy is a grown man. He'd probably jump at the chance to run the organization without your dad to interfere."

"Sammy wouldn't refuse to work with us out of loyalty to my father so much as he'd refuse in order to protect himself. If anyone thought he was on the side of the cops, he wouldn't have any power, even with my father out of the way. And he could think that this would be letting the police get a wedge in. First, they take out his father, then they start in on him. He wouldn't risk it."

"Then what else can we do? Sammy is all we've got."

"I've been thinking about that." She sat up straighter, water streaming off her shoulders and the tops of her breasts, distracting him. "There's somebody else we can lean on to try to find out where my father is staying," she said.

He forced his attention back to her face. "Who's that?"

"His driver. He always has one. He's not going to ride a shuttle like a common tourist, and he doesn't drive himself. Instead, he has a car take him from wherever he's staying, and drop him off at the base of the lifts. If we find the driver, we can either follow him back to the hideout, or we can try to persuade him to tell us the location of the house."

"Talking is probably better than following. He's

liable to spot a tail and get suspicious. Outside of town, there isn't much traffic."

"Tomorrow morning, we should go to the drop-off area near the gondola and look for the driver. We might even see my father, which would confirm he's here."

"Have I told you lately that you're brilliant?"

"Not brilliant enough to think of it before now."

"That's still brilliant." He checked the elevator again; no one had come up. They were still alone. "Patrick Thompson is worried about you," he said.

"He takes his job seriously."

"Because he's in love with you?" Thompson had denied any romantic feelings for Anne, but maybe she felt more deeply for the man who had rescued her from possible death.

She regarded him coolly. "Why? Are you jealous?"

"Yes."

"Jake, don't." She put up a hand as if to physically push him away.

"I know things can't be the way they were between us before," he said. "But I want you to know, it meant a lot to me when you told Thompson you trusted me."

"I do trust you, Jake. I'm just—we're both different now."

"I know. Just trust that I'm here if you need me—for whatever."

She nodded and looked away. He wanted to reach across the foaming water and pull her to him, but he held back. He cared about her, but maybe some of what he felt for her was merely nostalgia for what they'd had once before. She had been right when she'd said they were different now. He didn't know if he had it in him anymore to trust anyone the way he'd once trusted her.

The elevator opened, and a trio of young women emerged, giggling and talking, robes open over bright bikinis. They headed straight for the hot tub. Jake stifled a groan. So much for quiet relaxation. He turned to suggest they leave, and found Anne moving toward him. Before he could say a word, she covered his mouth with hers, and wrapped her arms around him. All coherent thought fled as he responded. For whatever reason, Anne was suddenly kissing him as if her life depended on it.

Chapter Fourteen

Jake's lips against Anne's felt both wonderfully familiar and excitingly new, she thought as she moved in closer. He wrapped strong arms around her and pulled her onto his lap, where the evidence of his desire pressed against her thigh, sending an almost-forgotten thrill through her. He slid one hand down her back to cup her bottom, and the thrill coalesced into full-on desire. She squirmed closer, and deepened the kiss, tasting him, unable to get enough of him.

"Ewww. Get a room!" a high-pitched voice said, followed by a chorus of giggles. Then the voices moved away.

Jake pulled back, just enough to slide his mouth to her ear. "Not that I'm sorry in the least, but what brought this on?" he asked.

"I didn't want those girls disturbing us."

"Mmmm." He nibbled her ear, and pure, erotic pleasure shivered through her. "Now you're the one who has me disturbed." He moved his mouth back to hers and kissed her again, a deep, shuddering kiss that left her breathless and clinging to him, as if he'd turned her bones to butter.

"I...I was just trying to get them to go away." She tried to move out of his arms, but he held her fast.

"So you were just acting. You didn't really want to kiss me." He traced the hollow of her neck with his tongue.

"Maybe I did." Maybe she'd wanted to kiss him since that first night in Rogers, when he'd held her in his arms. "I just don't know if this is a good idea." Why start something they couldn't finish?

"I think it's a very good idea." He cupped her bottom more tightly, and slid one finger into the leg opening of her swimsuit.

She gasped. "I..." But words failed her as he slipped one finger into her. He moved his other hand up to cup her breast, rubbing his palm over the sensitive nub of her nipple.

"Do you remember that night after your father's birthday party?" he asked. "When we sneaked out to the pool after everyone was asleep?"

She had a sudden vision of moonlight on water, the cityscape behind them. Moonlight on the hard planes and honed muscles of Jake's lithe body, naked as he dove into the water. She'd been naked, too, bold as she swam after him, then with him. They'd teased and tantalized each other, unashamed, then made love on a chaise longue by the edge of the water, no doubt providing entertainment for the guards who remained unseen, but whom she knew were on duty. Guards were always on duty in her father's house.

"Th-that was Elizabeth," she stammered, as he moved his finger to stroke her. "I'm Anne now."

"And Anne doesn't do things like this?" He bent his

head and covered her breast with his mouth, kissing her through the thin, wet fabric of the suit.

"Jake, we can't." She put both hands on his shoulders and pushed him away. She retreated across the hot tub and wrapped her arms across her chest. "I shouldn't have done that," she said. "I'm sorry."

"I'm not." His eyes burned into her. "We can go up to the room and finish this."

She swallowed hard, fighting the images his invitation suggested, of naked bodies writhing in the sheets, of Jake doing things to her he did so well. "I don't think that would be a good idea."

"Is that your brain or your heart talking?"

"Jake, I don't love you anymore. I can't."

"Can't—or won't?"

"It's too dangerous." She'd seen him die on that ballroom floor, bleeding to death in front of her, and for a while she hadn't wanted to live, either. She couldn't go through something like that again.

"Don't tell me you don't still want me," he said.

"Yes, I want you. But…" Heat suffused her cheeks and she almost laughed. After all they'd done, to think she could still be embarrassed. "I haven't been with anyone in over a year."

"No one since me, you mean?" His voice grew husky. "I haven't been with anyone, either."

It would be so easy to move back into his arms, to give in to the longing that thrummed in every fiber of her being. To forget, for a blissful hour or so, about the danger that surrounded them and the uncertain future that loomed before them.

But the events of the past year had proved the folly of ever taking the easy route, or of letting emotion get the upper hand over sense. "I can't start something with you that we can't finish," she said. "I'm not that reckless anymore."

"Then I'll be reckless enough for both of us," he said.

"You know that's not wise."

"Since when was I ever a wise man? Especially where you're concerned."

"You're one of the smartest men I know. Right now we need to concentrate on staying alive and finding my father."

His expression grew pained. "You're right, but it doesn't make me happy to admit it."

She'd once believed her job was to make herself happy, that everything would fall into place if she just focused on that. Her self-indulgence had almost gotten Jake killed, and had destroyed the life she'd known.

"I'd better go in," she said.

Not waiting for his answer, she climbed out of the tub and slipped back into her robe and boots. As she crossed to the elevator, the three bikini-clad girls descended on him. She fought back a stab of jealousy. Maybe those girls were just what he needed to take his mind off her. She was determined not to complicate matters by getting involved with Jake again, but she wasn't so strong she wouldn't spend time mourning what might have been.

THE NEXT MORNING, Jake and Anne were at the drop-off area at the base of the gondola at eight-thirty. The lifts opened at nine, and Anne said her father liked to get an early start, to beat the crowds and get the best lines in the freshly groomed snow and unpacked powder.

Neither of them had said a word about their exchange

in the hot tub, though Jake couldn't stop thinking about it. His skin still felt feverish from her touch, and he'd spent a restless night fantasizing about making love to her, hearing her scream his name in delight the way she used to.

For the hundredth time, he shoved the fantasy away. He had work to do. And she was right—he couldn't afford to let himself get distracted.

From a table on the balcony of a coffee shop that overlooked the drop-off area, they watched a procession of SUVs, shuttle buses and sedans drop off skiers and snowboarders. A figure in red pants and a red jacket, his short-cropped white hair shining in the sun, crossed the courtyard on his way to the lift. "That's Senator Nordley," Jake said.

Anne studied the stocky man, who'd paused to speak with a trio of women near the lift. "He doesn't look familiar," she said. "I don't think he was ever at the house while I was there."

"It would be interesting to follow him and see what he does while he's here."

"He probably skis, and hits the bars and the shops, like everyone else who comes here on vacation," she said. "And you're supposed to be looking for my father, not politicians."

"Right." Just then, a black four-door sedan pulled into the line. He and Anne both leaned forward. "Is that him?" Jake asked.

"I don't know yet," she whispered, though there was no chance the occupants of the vehicle would hear her from up here.

The car eased into position at the head of the line and the back door opened. A man dressed in black ski pants and a black and white jacket slid out, followed by a second man, who went around to the trunk and took out two pairs of skis.

The first man looked up at the gondola, and for a moment the sun caught him full on the face. Anne gave a small cry, and Jake put his hand on her arm to steady her. "That looks like him, doesn't it?" he asked.

She nodded. "Yes."

Jake studied the man more closely. He was trim, and tanned, silver hair showing beneath a black watch cap. Sunglasses shaded his eyes, but Jake remembered Sam Giardino's intense blue gaze. Even from this distance, dressed in ski clothes, Sam radiated command. He strode toward the gondola, the man with him shouldering both pairs of skis. The car pulled away from the drop-off area, into the line of vehicles waiting to exit.

"Come on, we'd better get down there." Jake stood and Anne followed him down the stairs and across the cobblestoned courtyard.

They'd discussed the plan last night and decided Anne would approach first—a tourist asking directions. While she had the driver distracted, Jake would make his move.

She hurried to the driver's door. Jake wiped the sweat from his palms and gripped the pistol inside his coat pocket. The last thing he wanted was a shootout here, with all these people around, but if the driver tried anything with Anne...

She knocked on the driver's window. Waited. Knocked again. Jake's chest hurt from holding his breath. Maybe this wasn't going to work.

Finally, the driver's window lowered. Anne was supposed to play the role of the pretty, flirtatious tourist, buying time for Jake to slip in and surprise the driver. But the smile on her face vanished when she saw the driver. She covered her mouth with one hand, and used the other to brace herself against the car. Then she opened the passenger door behind the driver and climbed in.

The car inched forward in the line of departing vehicles. Anne was being driven away by a killer—or at least by a killer's employee. This definitely wasn't part of their plan. Gripping the gun in his pocket, Jake sprinted toward the car. Anne leaned forward and said something to the driver and the door locks clicked. When Jake tried the door, it was open, so Anne must have told the driver to let him in.

"Mr. Westmoreland. I'm surprised to see you here." The driver looked at Jake in the rearview mirror, his expression hidden by dark glasses.

Jake leaned forward and pressed the muzzle of the gun against the back of the driver's neck. "Drive us to the overlook just outside of town. Pull in there."

Anne stared at him, eyes wide. "Jake! This is Doug. He used to drive me to school when I was a little girl. He would never hurt me. Put that gun away."

"Your father wants you dead, and he works for your father."

"I'm a driver, not a killer." Doug put the car into gear and turned onto the street that led away from the ski resort. "I'm glad to see Miss Elizabeth looking so well, but I can't say the same about you."

"Jake isn't with the feds anymore," Anne said. "He's just trying to protect me."

"No offense, Miss Elizabeth, but I always thought

you could do a lot better than the likes of him. I thought so the first day you brought him home."

"I didn't ask for your opinion." Jake shoved the gun harder against the chauffeur's neck. He recognized the man now, a weathered, reedy sixtysomething, who chewed spearmint gum nonstop and did Sudoku puzzles while he waited for Sam to summon him.

"Jake, please." Anne put a hand on Jake's arm, but he shrugged her off. She wanted him to be gentle with the old chauffeur, but these people didn't deserve gentleness. They only understood violence.

Doug removed his sunglasses and his eyes met Jake's in the rearview mirror. Clearly, he thought Jake was the equivalent of something he'd wipe off the bottom of his shoe, but he had apparently decided to humor him, for Elizabeth's sake. He put the car in gear and drove toward the overlook. No one said anything, though Jake could feel Anne beside him, disapproval radiating from her like strong perfume.

The paved pullout overlooking the town was empty. Doug nosed the car up to the rock wall that separated visitors from the canyon below and shut off the engine. "We're here," he announced.

"Anne, get out of the car and leave us," Jake said.

"No." She glared at him. "I won't let you hurt him." She turned to Doug. "I want to see my father," she said. "Please tell us where he's staying."

"You know I can't do that, Miss Elizabeth. I'd do almost anything for you, but I can't do that."

"Tell us where Giardino is staying, or I'll blow your head off." Jake cocked the gun. Anne gasped, but he ignored her. Anger made his pulse pound and formed a painful knot in his chest. After so many months of suffering and planning, he was finally close to the people who had caused him so much pain—people who had hurt Anne and destroyed her life. He was a professional; he would control himself. But that didn't mean he didn't long for a little revenge.

Sweat dotted the driver's forehead, but he remained calm, eyes fixed on Anne. "I can't tell you where Mr. Giardino is staying," he said. "But I can give him a message from you, if you'd like."

"No!" Jake barked, before Anne could answer. The tears that shimmered in her eyes made him feel about two inches tall. He gentled his voice. "If he knows you're here, he'll send someone to kill you."

"He must know I'm in the area," she said. "He sent those other men after us."

"If you care anything about her at all, you won't betray her to her father," Jake told the driver.

Doug nodded, the barrel of the weapon scraping the soft flesh of his neck, making a red mark.

"Tell Sammy I'm here and I want to see him," Anne said.

Jake sent her a questioning look, but she avoided his gaze.

"Where will he find you?" Doug asked.

"Tell him she'll meet him at the bar at the base of the gondola in town tonight at seven," Jake said. The bar was public enough Sammy probably wouldn't try anything, yet they'd be able to have a private conversation.

Doug nodded. Anne looked sick, but she nodded, too.

The sound of an old-fashioned telephone ringing made Jake flinch, though he kept the gun steady. "That's my cell," Doug said.

The ringing sounded again, out of place in the morning stillness. "Answer it," Jake said.

Doug picked up the phone. "Hello... Yes, Mr. Giardino. I'll be right there."

He clicked off the phone and looked at Anne. "That was your father. He forgot his neck gaiter and wants me to bring it to him. Do you want to come with me and see him now?"

She hesitated. Jake wanted to tell her no, but he held his tongue. She knew what was at stake here.

She shook her head. "No. I won't see him now. Just... just give Sammy my message." She sagged back in the seat. "Please drop us off before you get to the gondola."

Ignoring Jake, despite the gun that was still pressed to the back of his neck, Doug started the car again, and pulled onto the highway.

"Drop us at the grocery store on the edge of town," Jake said.

"Miss Elizabeth?"

"Yes. The grocery store is fine." Anne hugged her arms across her chest and stared out the window, her expression distant, her face pale. No doubt she'd have plenty to say to Jake later. Fine. Let her be angry with him; anger wouldn't stop him doing whatever he had to in order to keep her safe.

Doug pulled the car into a space at the edge of the grocery store parking lot. "It was good to see you, Miss Elizabeth," he said.

"It was good to see you, too, Doug."

"Take care of yourself."

"I will."

"I'll give Mr. Sammy your message."

"Thank you."

Jake stowed the gun in his coat and followed Anne out of the car. As soon as he shut the door behind them, Doug pulled away. Anne wrapped her coat more tightly around her and angled her body away from Jake. "I thought you didn't think Sammy would help us," he said.

"But he's all we've got, isn't he?" She whirled to face him, anger restoring some of the color to her face. "If you hadn't pulled that gun and started making threats, I could have talked Doug into telling me what we need to know."

"Or, he'd have pulled his own gun and marched you straight to your father."

"I couldn't let you hurt Doug. I thought if I did what you wanted in the first place—agree to talk to Sammy—you'd let the old man alone."

He leaned close, almost, but not quite touching, his voice low, his gaze locked to hers. "I know this is hard for you. These people are your family. But you know they're also killers. And I will do anything—including risking your anger—to protect you from them."

The resentment was gone now, replaced by grief and resignation. "I know." She stared at the icy pavement beneath their feet. "Maybe Sammy will help us. You were right when you said there's no love lost between him and my father. Things may have gotten worse since I left."

"Are you okay?" He studied her face, trying to read her emotions, but she refused to meet his gaze. So much for thinking he'd fully gained her trust.

"I'm scared," she said after a moment. "Scared this trip is a waste of time and I'm going to have to run away again. Scared we've somehow made things worse."

"I won't give up until I find your father," he said. "I won't leave this alone until you're safe."

He started to pull her into his arms, but stopped as a black SUV braked to a stop in front of them, so close it almost brushed against them. The front passenger window lowered and Sammy Giardino looked out at them. "Doug told me you wanted to see me," he said. "No reason to wait until tonight when I'm right here."

Chapter Fifteen

Anne stared at Sammy, feeling as if she'd been thrust into a dream—one of those she'd had often in the early days of her exile, in which she ran into a member of her family on the street. The dreams had various outcomes—sometimes the other person embraced her, sometimes they turned away. In the worst dreams, they came at her with knives or guns. But Sammy did none of those; he merely regarded her calmly. Without his ski helmet and goggles, he looked more like the young man she remembered—a twenty-five-year-old version of their father, dark-haired and black-eyed, with the same hooked nose and square jaw that made Sam Giardino look so intimidating.

"Hello, Sammy," she said, trying to keep the shakiness from her voice. "You're looking well."

"And you look like a schoolteacher." He wrinkled his nose. "Where did you get those clothes—a thrift store?"

Was he goading her because he knew the answer to that question? Had he been aware of her the whole time she'd been in town? No, it was just a logical guess. The fact that it was all true was just a coincidence. "How have you been?" she asked.

"Well enough." Behind them, a car honked. Sammy

glanced around the crowded parking lot. "This isn't exactly the right place for a private conversation. You must have a hotel room or something we can go to."

"You don't need to know where she's staying." Jake spoke up. Tension radiated from him, and he regarded Sammy with obvious suspicion. Anne knew the hand he kept in his coat pocket rested on his gun; she hoped Sammy wouldn't be foolish enough to try anything here in this public place.

"It's all right." She turned back to Sammy. "I'm staying at the Columbia. Meet us there in the lobby and we'll go up to my room together."

"I'll give you a ride." He hit the button to unlock the car doors.

"We'll walk." Jake took her arm. "And come alone." Not waiting for an answer, he pulled Anne away.

As soon as they were out of the grocery store parking lot, she jerked out of his grasp. "I don't appreciate being bullied," she said.

"Then I'm not the man you need to worry about right now. What are you doing, letting him know where you're staying?"

"We need somewhere private to talk. And we need to get Sammy to trust us. We can't do that if we don't at least pretend we trust him. If you don't think it's safe, we can change hotels after he leaves."

She expected him to argue with her, but he merely took a deep breath and nodded. "All right. But we need to be careful. We don't know if he's on our side yet. If we can't persuade him to help us, we'll have to leave town in a hurry. And I hope you have Thompson's number on speed dial."

"It will be all right. You'll see." She couldn't believe

her brother would hurt her—but then, she never would have believed her father would want her dead. The events of the past year had made her wary of her own instincts.

"I won't leave you alone with him," Jake said.

The words made her feel stronger. "And I won't leave you alone with him, either." She smiled, trying to lighten the mood, but his expression remained grim.

"I'm not the one he's liable to hurt," Jake said.

"Don't be too sure of that. In case you haven't noticed, my family doesn't have a lot of fond feelings for you."

"Was it like that before, and I didn't know it? Or did finding out I worked for the FBI taint their opinion of me?"

"What do you think? If I'd known you were with the Bureau, I wouldn't have come within ten feet of you." She smiled to soften the sharpness of her words.

"But now my irresistible charm and sex appeal have overcome those reservations."

His tone was teasing, but the heat of his gaze made her heart pound and her breath catch, especially as she remembered how close she'd come yesterday to giving herself to him once more. If only life were less complicated, and love was simply a matter of acting on feelings, without worrying about the consequences of those actions.

Sammy was already waiting when they reached the hotel, standing under the portico, hands in his jacket pockets, his expression somber and unreadable as he watched them approach. Did he see the big sister he'd once adored, or the traitor who had destroyed the family? "I sent my driver away," he said. "So it's just me. And no one else knows I'm here."

"Thank you. It's better for all of us if we're careful."

She led the way to the elevator, Jake bringing up the rear. He and Sammy hadn't exactly been friends when they'd known each other before; she suspected Sammy had been jealous of this other young man who had claimed her father's attention.

When she started toward her room, Jake moved up beside her and took the card key from her hand, then moved past her door to his. His gallantry touched her, though she thought it was unnecessary. If Sammy really wanted to know where she was staying, she had no doubt he could find out. But she said nothing and let Jake lead the way.

She waited until they were in the room with the door shut before she spoke. "How have you been, Sammy? And how are Stacy and Carlo?"

"Carlo is getting big, talking up a storm. Stacy still hates my guts, but nothing new about that."

"I'm sorry to hear that," Anne said. She knew her brother's marriage had been more a business arrangement than a love match, but she'd hoped with time the couple would be happier.

"What about you? Please tell me you haven't gone and married this scum." He scowled at Jake.

"Don't hold back, Sammy," Jake said. "Let us know how you really feel."

"I never liked you from the moment I laid eyes on you," Sammy said. "You were too cocky by half. It was bad enough you fooled Elizabeth, but then you had the old man believing your lies. I thought the one good thing to come out of that night was that we were rid of you."

"Sammy, stop it." Anne stepped between the two men. "I didn't invite you here to listen to you two bicker with each other."

"Then why did you want to see me?" He sat in the room's only chair and crossed his arms over his chest. He was a big, powerful man, and the posture only emphasized this. Anne had a hard time seeing the little boy he'd once been in the muscular, scowling figure before her. She'd counted on his fond feelings for her swaying him to her position, but now she wondered if that was even possible, especially given his antagonism toward Jake.

"I was hoping you'd tell me where Sam and the others are staying," she said.

"Why? So your boyfriend can swoop in and finish what he started a year ago?"

That was why they were here, but she didn't think stating it so boldly would help their case. The key to dealing with Sammy, ever since he was a toddler who wanted to stay up past his bedtime, was to persuade him to see how doing what you wanted would benefit him. First, she had to get past his animosity for Jake. "Jake isn't my boyfriend. Until recently I thought he was dead. And he doesn't work for the FBI anymore."

"Then what are you doing with him? And why are you here in Telluride?"

Jake was here for revenge—but why was she here? Not to rekindle her romance with Jake. They'd already agreed that wasn't possible. But being with him had reminded her of all she was missing by hiding from life.

"I'm tired of running away," she said. "Tired of

living a lie. I want to be able to go places and meet people without always looking over my shoulder. You can help me."

He looked wary. "How can I do that?"

"Tell us where Sam is. Help us put him in prison again."

"He'll just get out. He has powerful friends in high places."

"Is Senator Nordley one of those friends?" Jake asked.

"What's it to you, Mr. Not-a-Fed?"

"I still have contacts in the Bureau."

"It doesn't matter who my father's friends are, just know that he's got them."

"They're closing in on your father's benefactor, whether it's Nordley or someone else," Jake said. "He won't be able to help the Giardinos much longer."

"I didn't ask Sammy here to talk about all that," Anne said. She put her hand on her brother's shoulder. "Did you know Sam is trying to kill me? He's sent people after me three times now."

"Three times and you're still alive?" Sammy uncrossed his arms and looked her up and down. "You're either very good or very lucky. I'm thinking lucky."

"You think it's all right that your father is trying to murder your sister?" Jake's voice rose; Anne feared he was in danger of losing his temper.

"You make it sound like a Greek tragedy." Sammy shrugged. "But in a way, I guess it is. She betrayed the family honor, so now she has to die."

His words sent a chill through her. "Is that really how you think?" she asked. The idea that even Sammy could regard her with such coldness filled her with immense sadness.

He shook his head. "My opinion doesn't count. Ask Pop—he'll tell you that."

"If your father is back in prison, where he belongs, you'll be head of the family," Jake said.

"And then you can come after me."

"I don't have a beef with you."

"Yet." He turned his attention back to Anne. "Are you sure Pop is behind these attempts to off you?"

"I recognized one of the men as having worked for him. And you heard him in court. He said I was dead to him, and he'd make sure that was the case."

"He said that in court because he was furious at being taken in. Since then, he's calmed down a lot."

"What do you mean, calmed down?" Sam had always had a volatile temper, and he was not a man prone to forgiveness. Anne could think of more than one person who'd met with an "unfortunate accident" after incurring her father's wrath; no doubt there were many more she didn't know about.

"Now you're the prodigal daughter," Sammy sneered. "You're his darling Elizabeth who could do no wrong. You were led astray by that FBI scum. And you never meant for things to turn out the way they did."

"He said those things about me?" she asked. "Really?"

"Only a hundred times. And in the next breath he's telling me how worthless I am. Why couldn't I be the one who went away, and not his darling Elizabeth?"

"So you're saying he doesn't want me dead?" She fought back the surge of hope that threatened to overtake her.

"I'm saying he doesn't talk like he wants you dead."

He turned to Jake. "He'd gladly see you in hell, though. If he finds out you survived the attack last year, you'd better watch your back."

"So he doesn't know I'm alive?" Jake asked.

"He never mentioned it. And I think he would have." He grinned at Jake, a horrible smile that made Anne shudder. "Maybe I should take you out—earn some points with Pop."

Jake never flinched. "Why mess up your clean record? The feds don't have anything on you. They don't have any reason to come after you once your father's out of the way."

"Except I'm a Giardino and they've got it in for us."

"No one has it in for you, Sammy." Anne began to pace back and forth in front of her brother. "I'm the one people are trying to kill."

"And I told you, I really don't think Pop is the one who's out to get you."

She stopped. He sounded so certain. And part of her wanted more than anything to believe that her father did not want her dead. "Then who is after me?"

"I can't answer that. But maybe the feds think you're a risk and they've decided it would be an easy out to kill you and make your death look like a mob hit."

"Sammy, that's crazy! The government has gone to a lot of trouble to put me in the Witness Security Program and keep me safe. Why kill me now?"

"Since when do the things the government does make sense?" He turned to Jake. "But don't you think it's suspicious how *he* showed up in your life again just about the time all these attacks started happening?"

Anne wrapped her arms around herself to ward off

a sudden chill. What Sammy was saying was preposterous. Jake had no reason to want to harm her. The
timing of his arrival and the attacks on her was just
coincidence. But Patrick had tried to warn her about
him, too.... Her eyes met his, and she saw the challenge there. Would she believe her brother, or her former lover?

"How do you know the attacks on your sister started
when I arrived?" Jake asked.

"I'm sure she mentioned it," he said.

"But I didn't," Anne said.

"You did," Sammy said. "How else would I have
known?"

How else, indeed? "What else do you know about
the attempts on my life?" she asked.

"Nothing. Pop only tells me things he thinks I need
to know, which is almost nothing."

"But you said your father wasn't behind these attempts to kill your sister," Jake said.

Sammy squirmed, and Anne was reminded of a time
when he was nine, and had been caught stealing change
from their father's desk. "I'm punishing you because
you took the money," her father had said, as he removed
his belt and prepared to give Sammy a whipping. "But
I'm throwing in a few extra licks because you need to
learn to be a better liar." Family values, Giardino style.

"I don't think Pop wants Elizabeth dead," Sammy
said. "That's all I know."

"We're not getting anywhere with this." Jake turned
to Anne. "Tell your brother to leave. We never should
have bothered him."

"I didn't say I wouldn't help." Sammy stood. "But I

think before you go in with guns blazing, you should come and talk to Pop. Make your peace with him. When you see he's no threat to you, you'll have no reason to turn him in."

Except for the fact that he was a killer who'd broken the law, she thought, but she didn't dare say the words out loud.

"That's the worst idea I've heard all year," Jake said. "Once she goes to her father, he'll have her. It's like asking her to volunteer to show up at her execution."

"I told you he won't hurt her. Are you calling me a liar?"

The two men glared at each other, two bulldogs arguing over a bone. But ultimately, this was her decision to make, wasn't it? "If I did go and talk to Sam— Pop—could you guarantee my safety...and Jake's?"

"You'll be safe. I'd be a fool to make any promises where Jake's concerned."

"Fine. Then I'll go by myself."

"No, you won't," Jake said.

"I have to do this, don't you see? I have to find out how my father really feels about me."

"He could kill you."

"I believe Sammy. He has no reason to lie to me."

"I can think of half a dozen reasons," Jake said.

"Watch it." Sammy moved toward them.

"Stop it! Both of you." She turned to Sammy. "Can you set up a meeting? Soon?"

He nodded. "I can send a car for you tomorrow."

"Give us the address and we'll come in our own car," Jake said.

Sammy shook his head. "And risk you tipping off the feds? No way. I'll send a car. And Elizabeth comes alone—without you or anybody else. And if we catch anyone tailing our car, there'll be hell to pay."

"All right," Anne answered before Jake could object again. "But Jake will be waiting for me, and if I don't check in with him every thirty minutes, he'll contact the U.S. Marshals office."

"I don't like it," Jake said.

"It's not your decision to make." To soften her words, she went to him and put one hand on his chest. "This is the only family I have. If I can find a way to make peace with them, I have to risk it."

He studied her face, as if something there might help him understand. Finally, he nodded. "If you're going to do this, then I'm going to do what I can to protect you."

"If you lovebirds are done with your little tête-à-tête, I'll go now." Sammy moved toward the door. "I'll call you here at the hotel and let you know what time."

"Are you going to tell Pop ahead of time that I'm coming?" she asked.

"Are you kidding? I wouldn't pass up the chance to have him thank me for bringing back his favorite child."

She followed him to the door, Jake close behind them. "I still can't believe you'd trust a fed," Sammy said as he stepped into the hall. "Or that he'd trust you."

"Why wouldn't I trust her?" Jake asked.

"After the way she betrayed you? If a woman did that to me, I know I wouldn't be so forgiving."

"Betrayed me?" Jake sent Anne a puzzled look.

"Sammy, I don't think—" she began.

He grinned—that horrible, gloating smile that didn't quite reach his eyes. "You mean he doesn't know?" He nudged Jake. "Your girlfriend here is the one who gave you up to Pop. She's the reason you almost died that night."

Chapter Sixteen

Anne waited until her brother had stepped into the elevator down the hall before she shut and locked the door of the hotel room. She could feel Jake's gaze on her, burning into her back. Her stomach churned and she had trouble taking a deep breath. Sammy was a fine one to talk of betrayal; the obvious delight he took in revealing her secret to Jake wounded her almost as much as her father's turning his back on her that day in court.

She forced herself to face Jake once more. His expression was grim, lines of strain deepening around his eyes. "Is it true?" he asked. "Did you betray me to your father?"

"Not deliberately. Though, in the end, the result was the same."

He crossed his arms over his chest, his posture rigid. "Tell me," he said.

How many times over the last year had she revisited that fateful day? How often had she played the depressing game of "what if?" What if she'd never spent that night at Jake's apartment? What if she'd never said what she had to her father? What if she'd been smarter, or shown more discretion, or at least hadn't been so trusting...

"Do you remember when I spent the night at your place, two days before the party where you were shot?" she asked.

"Yes." His voice were clipped, his expression wary.

"Then you remember how you went downstairs to get takeout from the deli on your building's ground floor." She forced herself to continue. "I stayed behind to wait."

"You didn't want to get up and get dressed," he said. "So you waited for me in bed. Naked."

She shivered, as if chill air had just crossed her bare skin, though the room was warm, and the look he gave her heated, despite the anger she sensed that lay just beneath the surface. "I decided to fix us a drink, so I got up and went into the kitchen. I found a bottle of wine that looked good, so I started looking through drawers for the corkscrew."

"And you found something besides the corkscrew," he said.

"Yes." She met his gaze, silently pleading for understanding. "I found a mini digital recorder. I didn't play the recording or anything—I really didn't even think anything of it. I put it back in the drawer and kept searching until I located the corkscrew and opened the wine."

"And then I came back with dinner and we continued our evening together."

"Yes." They'd drunk the wine and eaten salad and calzones and made love until they were both sore and sated. She closed her eyes against the images her mind insisted on replaying—of Jake, naked and reaching for her, a look of such tenderness and passion in his eyes it still left her trembling.

"I don't understand what this has to do with your supposed betrayal," he said.

She opened her eyes again. "The next day, I was in my father's office at our apartment. I was looking for a stamp to mail a thank-you note and he was complaining that the tape system he used to record all his phone calls was malfunctioning again. I told him he ought to get one of those mini digital recorders. It would take up so much less space and he wouldn't have to mess with tapes. He wasn't very tech savvy, and he didn't know what I was talking about, so I told him you had one— that you'd probably be glad to show him. It was small enough to put in your pocket and no one would ever even know it was there."

"And that made him wonder why I had a recorder that could be hidden so easily."

"Later, he came to me and started asking more questions—about what you did when you weren't with me, who your friends were, what else I'd seen at your apartment. I was confused, but I thought he was just being the typical overprotective father. I told him what I knew, but I truly didn't think anything of it. When I asked him why he was so interested, he told me not to worry, that he would take care of everything."

"Meaning, he would take care of me."

"If I'd had any idea what he was planning, I would have warned you, I swear. I never thought—" Her voice broke and she covered her face with her hands, reliving the horror of Jake bleeding to death in her arms. "I'm so sorry. When I think if all you suffered because of my foolishness…"

He closed the distance between them and put his arm

around her shoulders. "I believe you," he said softly. "You never meant for me to be hurt. For both of us to be hurt."

She curled into him, her face pressed into the hollow of his shoulder. Closing her eyes, she breathed in his scent—cotton and fabric softener, and the aroma of clean male skin that was uniquely him. It was the scent she associated with strength and safety and long nights of lovemaking.

"The worst days in the hospital, I would distract myself from the pain by trying to remember every detail of that evening—how you looked, what you said, the way you felt." He took her hand in his and trailed his thumb across her knuckles, tracing the ridges and valleys, his touch light but sending a jolt of awareness through every nerve.

A fierce desire stabbed her, a need to feel him around her and in her, affirming life in the most elemental way she knew. She raised her head and found his gaze fixed on her, his eyes reflecting the same wanting she felt. "Make love to me," she whispered.

He caressed the side of her neck, then trailed one finger along her jaw until it rested lightly against her bottom lip. "I've wanted to make love to you since the first night I saw you again," he said. "But are you sure?"

"I'm sure." She wrapped her hand around his, and kissed his fingertips. "I have no idea what's going to happen tomorrow, or the next day, or the day after that. All we can count on is now. And right now, I want to be with you."

"Then I'll stay. And I won't leave you until you tell me to go."

JAKE HELPED ANNE pull her sweater over her head, then steadied her as she stripped off boots and pants. He was glad of something to do to hide the trembling in his hands as he acted out the fantasy that had played in his dreams too long. When she stood before him, naked, he smiled, remembering how bold she'd always been with him before. For all the ways she'd been forced to change in the last year, she hadn't left that boldness behind.

She took hold of the waistband of his ski pants. "You're still dressed," she chided. "We must do something about that."

He unsnapped the pants, then hesitated. "I have a lot of scars from the shooting and the surgeries afterward," he said. "It's not a pretty sight."

"I saw a little yesterday and I didn't think you were too horrifying."

His face must have betrayed his dismay at her choice of words. She laughed and reached for him. "I'm not afraid of scars," she said. She grasped the tab of his zipper and slowly lowered it. His erection strained against the fabric, eager for her touch. As if answering the unspoken summons, she slipped her hand into his underwear and wrapped her fingers around his length. He pulled her close and lowered his mouth to hers in a fierce, claiming kiss.

Cupping her bottom, he pulled her tight against him, his erection pressed to her stomach, the soft fullness of her breasts flattened against the hard plain of his chest. Desire pulsed between them in time with their pounding hearts. After so long a time apart he forced himself to draw out the waiting a little longer, to savor the anticipation.

Her mouth still locked to his, she tugged at his pants

and underwear. He broke the kiss and quickly stripped out of the garments, and pulled his wool sweater and thermal top over his head. While his face was still buried in the tangle of clothing, she placed her hands over his ribs and began kissing her way around the puckered, white scar on his chest that marked a bullet's path. The touch of her lips was light, little more than a flutter, but he felt the kisses deep within, touching wounds he'd shied away from examining too closely, wounds of doubt and fear and loss, soothed by her tender caresses.

He grasped her by the shoulders and urged her to stand straight. "Let me look at you," he said.

She stood without shame, letting his gaze take in the full, firm breasts, indented waist and gently curved hips. She was thinner than she'd been before, her ribs standing out more, but she could have gained thirty pounds or lost twenty more and he wouldn't have cared. To him, she would always be beautiful, the one woman whose body fit him perfectly.

She traced her finger along a network of scars across his chest. "Are all of these from when you were shot?" she asked.

"Some of them are from surgery to remove the bullets, and a port for IV antibiotics to fight an infection."

Her gaze fell lower, to the scars on his legs. "I suppose you could always tell people you played football or something."

He laughed, as much from sheer happiness as anything else. "There's only one athletic pursuit I'm interested in at the moment," he said, pulling her close once more.

They moved to the bed, slipping between the crisp sheets to lie facing one another. She smoothed her hands down his side, fluttering her fingers along his ribs and coming to rest on his hips. "Every time with you is new," she said. "And yet so familiar."

"So right." He began kissing her again, tracing the line of her jaw, running his tongue along the tender flesh of her throat, relishing the swell of her breasts, and the way her breath caught as he drew the sensitive tip into his mouth. He nipped and licked and teased until she was breathless and writhing beneath him, her body arching upward in a silent plea that made his own desire quicken and intensify.

He moved lower still, to kiss her stomach, and the tender flesh of her inner thighs, and the softly furred mound between her thighs, stroking and coaxing while she moaned her delight. He ached for her, but refused to give in to that aching until he had shown her every pleasure.

She put her hands on his shoulders, urging him upward. "I want you in me," she pleaded.

"Your wish is my command." He moved his body alongside hers, then leaned over to open the drawer beside the bed.

"What are you doing?" she asked.

"I thought we needed this." He opened his palm to reveal the condom he'd taken from the drawer.

She smiled. "You think of everything."

"I try to be prepared."

"Were you so sure you'd get me into your bed?"

"I wasn't sure, but I wasn't going to let anything spoil the moment if I had the chance."

She held out her hand. "Allow me."

He handed her the packet and she tore it open and removed the condom, then knelt before him and rolled it on. He held his breath and tried to think of something mundane—multiplication tables or tax codes or anything else to keep him from flying apart as her hands closed around him.

Condom in place, he pushed her gently back against the pillows and knelt between her legs. She flashed a coy smile and reached down to guide him in, and then together they began to move in a dance whose moves they had not forgotten in a year apart. She smiled up at him, face suffused with joy as they increased their tempo, anticipation and tension building.

He slipped his hand between them to fondle her, and was rewarded with a breathy "Yes!" Her eyelids fluttered and her head fell back as passion overtook her. "Jake," she cried, then louder, "Jake!" A sound of triumph and completion as she tightened around him.

He held on for a few more thrusts, then surrendered to his own need, months of fear and worry and denial vanquished in the letting go.

They lay crushed together for a long moment, coming back to themselves, waiting for breath and heart to slow. At last, he rolled off of her, but she clung to him, pressing her face against his chest.

"What are we going to do, Jake?" she asked after a while, after he'd pulled the covers over them and was drifting toward sleep.

"What are we going to do about what?" He forced himself out of slumber, and smoothed his hand down her back, reassuring himself that yes, she was real, and this was no dream.

"About tomorrow, to start with. I know you don't think I should go with Sammy to see my father."

So reality would insist on intruding on this moment.

Well, that was what had brought them here, after all. "I don't trust Sammy," he said. "He was too smug. Too sure of himself."

"He was like that before—don't you remember? He's my father's son, and all the men in my family have that cocky attitude. It's all about power and control. Never let anyone see you sweat."

"He's jealous of you and of your relationship with your father." As much as he disliked Sammy, he didn't blame him for the jealousy. Even in Jake's brief time with the family, he'd seen the difference in the way Sam Giardino treated his children, spoiling his daughter and denying his son. "Maybe he thinks he can raise himself up in your father's eyes by delivering you to the old man on a platter."

"Maybe you're right. But my father loved me more than anything else in the world," she said.

"You said before that kind of love might turn to hate."

"Did your love for me turn to hate?" she asked.

"No." He kissed her forehead. "Never."

"I thought I could convince myself to hate you, but it turned out to be impossible." She settled her head against his chest once more. "Once I knew you were alive again, all my old feelings for you started growing again. I don't think you can ever turn off or put aside love like that."

"No, you can't," he agreed. Love like that could keep you going through hell. It could make life worth living—and make you miserable, sometimes at the same time. "And you still love him."

"Yes. In spite of everything, I do. If there's a chance to patch things up with him, I have to take it."

"And then what? You let him go on his way, back

to his life of crime? He welcomes you back into the family fold and you go back to being the pampered mafia princess?"

She rose up on one elbow, so she could look him in the eyes. "I could never go back to that life," she said. "I'd have to leave again, but at least I could do so knowing I still had a family. I still had a father who loved me, no matter how flawed he is."

"And after you leave, I'll have to bring in Thompson and his men to arrest your father. And your brother, too, if he tries to interfere." One thing he wouldn't do was lie to her—not ever again.

She nodded. "I know. And I'll admit part of me would feel guilty, but I've learned to live with guilt."

"Have you considered that your father might not let you leave?"

Her expression clouded. Clearly, she hadn't thought about this possibility. "He couldn't keep me prisoner," she said.

"I think he has the manpower and the resources to do whatever he wants," Jake said. "Including keeping his beloved daughter by his side forever—whether she wants to stay there or not."

She shook her head. "I wouldn't stay. I could never live like that again. He'd have to see—"

"I think your father has made a life out of seeing what he wants to see."

Her eyes met his, filled with sadness, but also determination. "You're probably right. If he tries to keep me with him, you should contact Patrick."

"I'd do that. But I wouldn't leave rescuing you up to the Marshals. I'd have to do what I could to save you."

"I'd be counting on it." She lay back down, nestled

against him once more, and he held her closely, wishing that was enough to protect her, to truly keep her safe.

He never heard her crying, but he felt the tears, hot and damp on his chest. He lifted her chin and his anxiety rose at the sight of wet tracks down her cheeks. "Why are you crying?"

She shook her head, smiling through the tears. "It's just… Why does the world have to be so screwed up?"

Why, indeed? He lay back, and cradled her head in the hollow of his shoulder. "Don't think about that now," he said. Soon enough, they'd have to face the future, a future that didn't hold any promise that they could be together. But worrying wouldn't change anything that was to come. Better to hold on to the present for a little bit longer.

Chapter Seventeen

Sammy called as Anne and Jake were finishing breakfast. She'd spent the night in his room, doing her best to savor the moments and not worry about the future. She could admit now—if only to herself—that she still loved Jake. But how could she ask him to give up everything to join her in hiding in witness protection? And if she left WitSec she doubted she'd fit into his life. Though he hadn't said, she suspected he had hopes of returning to a career in law enforcement; being linked to the daughter of a mafia don would make that ambition impossible to realize.

So it was with a heavy heart that she answered the phone and heard her brother's voice on the other end. "I'll pick you up in front of your hotel at ten-thirty," he said, then hung up before she could ask any questions.

"That was Sammy," she said as she replaced the phone in the cradle. "He says he'll be here at ten-thirty."

"Did he give you any idea of what your father thinks of this reunion?"

"No. He didn't say anything else." She studied the silent phone. "Maybe we should call Patrick."

"Maybe we should. He'll tell you the same thing I did—don't go. Will you listen to him?"

"If I don't go, I'll spend the rest of my life wondering what would have happened if I had." She took a deep breath and straightened her spine. *Courage*. "Besides, this is our best chance to pin down Sam's location. This is the closest anyone has come to him in a year." She forced a smile. "Once I've left the house, you'll be able to get him." They'd already discussed the possibility that her father might not allow her to leave. No sense bringing that up again. She'd deal with that problem if it presented itself.

"I know I said that's what I wanted," Jake said. "But it's not worth risking your life over."

"If I don't confront him I could lose my life anyway. He's either responsible for sending those men to kill me, or he knows who is."

Worry made Jake look ten years older. "I wish you'd let me come with you."

"You'd never even get into the car. I don't trust Sammy not to shoot you on sight."

She expected him to argue more, but he only nodded. "I'll be waiting for your calls. Every half hour or I'll send in the cavalry."

"Don't worry, I'll call." Just hearing his voice would give her the courage she'd need to get through this. She and Jake had both purchased new phones yesterday— cheap pay-as-you-go models that would allow them to keep in touch today. She stood. "I'd better get ready."

She took her time with her hair and makeup. Her father appreciated glamour in a woman, and though she didn't like to admit it, Sammy's comment yesterday about her looking like a schoolteacher had stung.

When she emerged from the bathroom shortly after

ten, Jake let out a low whistle. "You look gorgeous," he said, and pulled her to him.

"Don't smudge the makeup," she said, and offered her cheek for a kiss.

He squeezed her waist, and brushed his lips against one cheek. "You'd better go down," he said. "I'm going to watch from the lobby, just in case."

Promptly at ten-thirty, the black SUV pulled under the portico. Anne was surprised to see Sammy driving. People in her family seldom ventured out without a bodyguard. She opened the door and slid into the passenger seat.

"I see you didn't chicken out," he said as she fastened her seat belt.

"Did you think I would?"

"You never would have before, but it's been a year. No telling what kind of brainwashing the feds have been doing."

There was no right answer to an accusation like that, so she chose to ignore it.

"So what have you been up to for the past year?" Sammy asked. "The old man spent a fortune trying to track you down and came up with zilch."

"I thought you said he wasn't after me." Renewed fear that she was, in fact, on the way to her execution, rose up to paralyze her.

"He didn't want to kill you—he wanted to bring you home. Where he thought you belonged."

"Oh." She forced herself to look more relaxed, though her heart still pounded.

"So where have you been?" he asked. "Did they really give you a new name and everything?"

"Yes, they gave me a new name. And a new job and a house and car. It's a very well-organized program."

"I'll bet. But you're not going to share any details."

"I really don't think I should." She looked out the window, at the crowds moving toward the ski gondola or filling the shops along the town's main street. "How far is it to the house where you all are staying?"

"Not far." He hunched over the steering wheel, tapping out a jerky rhythm with his fingers as they inched through morning traffic. When a car somewhere behind them backfired, he jumped and swore.

"Is everything okay?" she asked.

"Why wouldn't everything be okay?"

"I don't know. You seem nervous."

"You're the one who should be nervous. Pop isn't going to be happy when he finds out you're still with Jake."

"I'm surprised you haven't already told him."

"I haven't told him anything. I told him I was bringing someone to see him this morning who he needed to talk to."

"So he doesn't know it's me."

Sammy grimaced. "I wanted it to be a surprise. One he'd remember me for."

A shiver went through her. Was Sammy intent on making a good memory, or a bad one?

"He won't like knowing about Jake, though," Sammy continued. "He'll probably send someone to take him out."

"I'm not 'with' Jake," she said. "I didn't even really want to come here with him, but he didn't give me much choice. I'll probably never see him again after this."

The lies rolled off her tongue, but she couldn't tell if Sammy believed her.

"Pop will be glad to hear it," he said. "Maybe with you back in the fold, he'll get off my back—though I doubt it. He always had a double standard where the two of us were concerned."

"You know I always took your side against him."

"You did. And he'd listen to you, when he wouldn't listen to me." He looked thoughtful, less agitated. Though she struggled to remain outwardly calm, her insides were roiling, heart pounding with fear—fear for her physical safety, yes. But also fear of being disappointed, of seeing her father look at her once more with hatred instead of love.

They left behind the last buildings of Telluride and turned onto a gravel county road that climbed into the mountains, past clusters of small houses and abandoned mine machinery. After a few more miles they turned onto a paved road that wound through acres of carefully positioned trees and miles of five-rail wooden fencing. She might have been looking at a painting entitled "A Colorado Estate in Winter."

In the distance, Anne spotted what appeared to be a gray stone castle set on a rise overlooking a broad valley. Twin turrets flanked a facade of glass and stone blocks that rose three stories, with two-story wings sprawling on either side of the main house. A separate three-car garage and various other outbuildings in matching stone dotted the grounds around the house. "Who owns this place?" she asked. "It's gorgeous."

"It belongs to a friend of Pop's. Somebody who wants him to partner in some business ventures."

Business ventures. It sounded so prosperous and

legitimate. Just another American capitalist doing his part to build a vital economy. Except that the Giardino family "businesses" always had the taint of the shady and illegal. Everything was shiny and respectable on the outside, but underneath was a layer of filth, too often tainted by blood.

They stopped at a stone guardhouse. A man dressed in black and openly cradling a semiautomatic rifle stooped to peer into the vehicle, then pressed a keypad to open the iron gate and waved them through.

A second armed man met them in front of the house and opened Anne's door. "Mr. Giardino is waiting for you," he said.

She smoothed the front of her coat, wishing she could as easily smooth down the butterflies in her stomach, and studied the entrance to the house, buying time. Stone columns rose three stories, supporting an arching portico in front of a fortune in stone and plate glass. She'd seen hotels that were less lavish. A massive chandelier made of hundreds of antlers strung with lights glowed from the top of the portico. A ten-foot oak-and-iron door stood open, providing a glimpse into a stone-floored foyer and more antler lighting.

Sammy moved up beside her and took her arm. "Come on," he said. "We don't want to keep Pop waiting."

"Of course not." In some ways, they'd both been waiting for this moment for the past year. There was no going back now, only forward. "Take no prisoners," she whispered to herself as she let her brother lead her into the house, and into her future.

"THEY'VE JUST TURNED onto a paved drive. The number on a post says five-twenty-four." Jake spoke softly into his phone, as if someone might overhear, though he was sitting in the battered Subaru alone, parked between a rusting ore cart and a leaning spruce, a quarter mile before the estate where Sammy had turned in.

"I've found it on our map." Patrick's voice was a low growl in Jake's ear. "Property belongs to a developer out of Denver, Jason Castle. Our friends at the ATF have had him on their radar for a while now, though they've never been able to make anything stick."

"I don't care about him," Jake said. "Can you get up there to look after Anne?"

"The place is guarded like a fortress. No way can we come in from the front."

"What about the back?"

"It's rugged country. You'd have to come in over the top of a mountain."

"What about a helicopter?"

"You obviously think I have a bigger budget than I do."

"Don't tell me the government wouldn't pull out all the stops to nail Sam Giardino."

"We still don't know for sure that he's there," Patrick pointed out.

"We know Anne's there. And she could be in danger."

"Then why did you let her go?"

"I had no right to stop her. Besides, what was I going to do—tie her up? Lock her in her room?"

"You could have tried harder to talk her out of going. You could have called me."

"I did call you. I'm talking to you now."

"Now that she's gone, there's not a lot I can do. You should have called me before."

"And you really think you could have talked Anne out of doing something she'd made up her mind to do?"

Thompson didn't answer. "What do you want me to do now?" he asked.

"I thought that was obvious. I want you to get a team in there to protect her."

"I'll see what I can do. It's going to take a little time to pull things together. Meanwhile, you stay put. I'll be in touch." He broke the connection.

Jake set his phone on vibrate, then took an extra ammunition magazine from the glove box and shoved it into the pocket of his ski jacket. He stowed his gun in the other pocket, pulled on a stocking cap and gloves, and climbed out of the car. He could just make out the snow-covered ridge of rock that rose up behind the massive stone house. Giardino and his men would never expect someone to come at them from that direction. Nothing but a mountain goat was likely to traverse that approach and live to tell about it.

He leaned back into the car and retrieved a county map he'd purchased from a local outdoor adventure supplier. In addition to roads, it showed all the Jeep trails, cross-country ski routes and hiking paths in the area. Jake traced the broken line of a path that led to the top of the peak behind the house. There was no corresponding trail down the other side, so he'd have to make his own. He glanced toward the house again. Anne's first call was due any minute now; he'd wait for it, then head for the mountains. One man against all of Giardino's thugs wasn't the best odds, but he'd have surprise on his side. And he'd promised Anne he'd protect her. It wasn't a promise he could afford to break.

SAMMY LED ANNE into the house, past more guards, who stood like armed statues on either side of the door leading into a great room with a twenty-foot ceiling and three stories of glass that looked out onto soaring mountain peaks. Two more guards waited inside the room, and regarded Anne and Sammy with blank expressions.

Patrick and his men would never get in here, she thought. Even if they found this place, they'd never get past her father's troops—not without an army of their own. She pushed aside her nervousness. She had to stay calm and keep thinking clearly. "Where's Pop?" she asked, looking around the room.

"He'll be here in a minute," Sammy said.

The alarm on her phone chimed. "I need to call Jake," she said. "If I don't check in, he'll be worried."

"Go ahead." Sammy nodded to her phone.

She hit the speed dial for Jake's new cell. He picked up on the first ring. "I'm here and I'm fine," she said. "This place is amazing." That was the code phrase they'd settled on to reassure him that everything was, in fact, okay.

"Have you see your father?" he asked.

"Not yet."

"Say goodbye now." Sammy moved over to her—close enough to snatch the phone away.

She fought the urge to stick her tongue out and turn her back on her brother, the way she would have when they were both teenagers. But she and Sammy weren't teenagers anymore, and as a grown man, second in command in the Giardino family, he had the power to do her real harm. "I'd better go now," she told Jake. "I'll call you again in half an hour."

She slid the phone back into her pocket. Sammy sank into an oversize leather chair and motioned for her to sit also. "Make yourself comfortable," he said. "Isn't this a fantastic place?"

"Very nice." She perched on the edge of a sofa that matched the chair. The room was full of overstuffed, oversize pieces, as if a race of giants lived here.

"Sammy! Do you have the lift tickets? I put them on the dresser and they're not there." An elfin woman with a cap of white-blond hair hurried into the room. She was dressed in a Nordic sweater, black leggings and short leather boots and was pulling on a pair of gloves as she spoke.

"Don't worry about the lift tickets," Sammy said. "You're not going skiing today."

"What do you mean I'm not—" She looked up, her voice trailing away in midsentence as she focused on Anne.

"What are you staring at?" Sammy asked. "Don't you recognize your own sister-in-law? Elizabeth is back with us."

All color fled from the face of the woman—Sammy's wife, Stacy. "What are you doing here?" she asked, her voice scarcely above a whisper.

"What kind of a question is that?" Sammy barked. "We're her family. Why shouldn't she be here?"

Stacy turned cold eyes on him. "I thought once she was lucky enough to get away, she'd be smart and never come back." She turned and left the room, her boot heels hitting hard on the plank floors as she hurried toward the stairs.

Sammy mumbled an obscenity under his breath as he watched his wife leave the room. "You should be nicer to her," Anne said—not for the first time.

"Why should I? She isn't nice to me."

"She'd probably respond better to kindness than cursing. And she's your wife. She's the mother of your son."

He grunted, his usual response to an argument he couldn't win.

The guards by the door snapped to attention, and Sammy rose to his feet. "What is it?" Anne asked, straining to see.

"Pop is here," he said. "I hope you're ready."

Her heart pounded, and she wanted to shout that she wasn't ready. But it was already too late. She stood also, and prepared to meet her father.

Chapter Eighteen

The trailhead that climbed the peak behind the estate where the Giardinos were hiding was a fifteen-minute drive from the road where Jake had been parked. He found the start of the trail without too much trouble, despite the snow. Fresh boot prints marked the route, and he wondered if they belonged to casual hikers or people who, like him, had come to check out the Giardino compound.

The trail was steep, but he powered up it, running until his lungs threatened to burst, then resting only long enough for his breathing to return to normal before he started up again. His legs, held together with pins in places, screamed in protest, but he ignored the pain. He had to get to Anne. No matter what Sammy said about her father being glad to see her, he didn't trust the Giardinos. They were a family of killers, and he didn't think they'd hesitate to kill one of their own.

After forty-five minutes of hard climbing, he came to the end of the trail at the top of the ridge, in a leveled-off area about five feet square, stamped clear of ice and snow. Someone had definitely spent time up here recently. Had Giardino sent some of his men up here to check out the approach? That would have been a smart move.

Or maybe the feds knew about this place and were keeping an eye on it. Thompson obviously knew more than he let on; Jake hoped the marshal would use his knowledge to save Anne.

He scanned the area below with binoculars. He counted four guards patrolling the perimeter, though they paid little attention to the back of the house, which was separated from a sheer natural rock wall by less than ten feet. The wall itself rose about twenty feet, and above that the mountain sloped back at what he judged to be a sixty-degree angle.

No doubt any scouts that had been sent up here to assess the situation had determined that approaching the house from this direction was impossible. Such an assault would require technical climbing equipment, not to mention nerves of steel.

Jake had been accused of having more nerve than sense, and he hadn't come this far to give up. He turned his back to the house and carefully lowered himself over the edge, gripping what rock he could with his hands, and feeling with his feet for the next best hold. Loose rock, icy slush and chunks of snow rained down, and it was impossible to determine stable footing from useless debris in the mix of snow, mud and ice that covered this aspect of the mountain. But he managed to advance a few feet.

At this rate, it would take him hours to reach Anne—hours she might not have. He should have purchased technical climbing equipment from that shop in town. But then, he'd have needed lessons in how to use it. This wasn't a skill the Bureau had bothered teaching in the classes he'd taken at Quantico.

It didn't matter. He couldn't see any other way to help Anne, so he kept on climbing, ignoring the pain and the fear and the voice inside his head that argued that no woman was worth risking his life this way.

But he didn't listen to the voice. He had promised Anne he'd do whatever it took to keep her safe, and it was a promise he intended to keep.

SAM GIARDINO STRODE into the room, looking more like Sammy's older brother than his father. Anne had imagined that the ordeal of a trial, prison time and escape, plus months evading recapture, would have aged her father, who was almost sixty. Instead, he looked younger than ever, his dark hair showing only a touch of gray at the temples, his tanned skin smooth and unlined. Hair dye and plastic surgery probably accounted for his youthful appearance, but whatever was behind the transformation, it sent a clear message that Sam Giardino was a long way from being counted out. He had the vigor and intelligence—and the power—of a much younger man.

Standing next to their father, Sammy looked soft and tired. His hair was thinning, his skin sallow, and he had the beginnings of a paunch, despite the powerful musculature of his chest and arms. Worse, Sammy lacked his father's attitude of command. He kept his gaze fixed on his father, alert for clues as to Sam's mood, and doing so gave him the attitude of a faithful dog who was trying to avoid being kicked.

Sam stopped halfway across the room, and studied his daughter with the burning blue gaze she remembered too well—a look that said if it was possible to read another person's thoughts, he would do so. "Elizabeth, is that really you?"

"Don't you recognize me?" she asked. She'd meant her tone to be defiant, but it came out in the voice of a lost little girl.

Then he opened his arms, the same gesture he'd used when she was a toddler heading toward him on unsteady legs, or a weeping preteen who'd been hurt by her first middle-school boyfriend. Those arms had been her refuge, a place of certain safety, and she could no more turn away from them now than she could then.

While Anne embraced her father, Sammy paced around them. "I tracked her down," he said. "I knew you'd want to see her."

Sam drew away, his expression solemn, but his eyes misty. "That was a good thing for you to do," he said. "Go tell Angie we will have an extra person for lunch. And she should fix something special. We have a lot to celebrate."

Sam's back was to his son, so he didn't see the scowl on Sammy's face when his father addressed him like an errand boy. But after a hard look at the older man, Sammy left the room, presumably to talk to the cook.

With his arm still around Anne, Sam led her to a sofa. "Come here and tell me why you stayed away a year."

The question was so preposterous she almost laughed out loud. "Dad, you swore you'd have me killed," she said. "I didn't think it was safe for me to come anywhere near you."

"And you were probably right, those first few months." His eyes met hers, the look chilling. "You did a very bad thing. An unforgivable thing. But a man gets weaker as he ages, and I wasn't strong enough to hold on to a hatred of you. Not having you in my life was worse than being in prison."

"Oh, Dad." She hugged him close and kissed his cheek. She wanted to believe his words, but doubt still nagged at her. She drew back.

"What is it?" he asked. "What's wrong?"

"A man came to my house last week—a man who used to work for you, DiCello. He tried to kill me."

"Frank DiCello left my employment six months ago," he said. "He went to work for an outfit in St. Louis, closer to his mother and sister."

"Then you didn't send DiCello after me?"

He looked genuinely puzzled. "No."

"He was wearing a lift ticket from Telluride on his jacket, so I thought he was here with you."

"I haven't seen DiCello since August."

"After the attack by DiCello, I hid out in a cabin in the National Forest," she said. "Someone set the cabin on fire while I was inside, sleeping. Later, on our way here, someone tried to run my car off the road."

"None of this has anything to do with me," Sam said. "I swear on my mother's grave."

This was the ultimate oath in the Giardino family, so Anne had no choice but to believe her father. "Then who is trying to kill me?" she asked.

Sammy returned. "Angie says lunch is in ten minutes," he said.

Sam's only reply was a nod. Tension stretched between father and son, worse than Anne remembered from before. She'd hoped, now that Sammy was older, her father would show him more respect, and give him more responsibility. But he still seemed to treat his only son like some low-level flunky.

The alarm on her phone beeped. "What was that?" Sam asked.

"I promised a friend I'd check in," she said.

"She needs to call Jake West," Sammy said. "You remember him, don't you, Pop? Though I take it these days he goes by his real name, Jacob Westmoreland."

"Jake West is dead," Sam said.

"We believed so, but turned out he's tougher than we thought." Sammy gripped Anne's shoulder, hard enough to make her flinch. "And it looks like he and Elizabeth here are still an item."

"Is this true?" Sam asked.

"It's true that Jake survived your attack on him. And that he came with me to Telluride." She chose her words carefully, wary of sending her father into a rage.

"Elizabeth still thinks she's in love with the guy," Sammy goaded.

"Is this true?" he asked again, her father's sharp gaze sending a shiver through her.

She opened her mouth to deny the words, but could not. Part of her did love Jake, even though she knew a relationship with him was impossible. "Jake is a good friend of mine," she said, and hoped she wasn't damning him with this faint praise.

"I meant it when I said I could never kill you," Sam said. "But Jake West is someone I would gladly kill—and I will, if I see him."

"Even if killing him hurts me?" she asked. Would she be able to live with herself if her father murdered Jake? Thinking about the possibility made it difficult to breathe.

"You'd be better off without a lying fed in your life," her father said with a sneer.

She swallowed hard. "I still need to call him, to let him know I'm okay."

Her father frowned, but said nothing, so she took out her phone and punched in Jake's number. After five rings, the call went to voice mail. "Leave a message," came the clipped recording in Jake's voice.

"This is Anne. I'm just checking in."

"You go by Anne now?" Her father gave her a curious look.

"Just…sometimes," she hedged. In the back of her mind, she could hear parts of Patrick's lecture on compromising her identity. But after today she'd have to start over again anyway, wouldn't she? Even if her father wasn't behind the recent attacks, someone was, and her luck against that unknown assailant wouldn't hold out forever. She'd have to question her father more later about who he thought might be after her.

A gong rang somewhere toward the back of the house. Her father took her hand. "It's time to eat," he said.

He led her to the dining room, another sunny space that looked out over the valley and the side of the estate. A long table, set with crystal and china, filled the center of the room. Sam took his seat at the head of the table. Anne sat on her father's right, across from an attractive, thirtysomething woman with long dark hair worn in a chignon, and the lithe body of a model or dancer. "This is Veronica. Veronica, this is my daughter, Elizabeth," her father said.

Anne nodded at what was probably her father's latest mistress. He'd had half a dozen such women in his life since her mother's death years before. They were all cast from the same mold—beautiful, classy and quiet. They voiced no opinions of their own and seldom joined in family conversations. When one left, to be replaced by a similar model, the rest of the family scarcely noticed.

Sammy occupied the other end of the table, with Stacy on his right and their son, Carlo, in a booster chair at her side. The boy, who had blond, curly hair and a winning smile that showed twin dimples, smiled shyly at his aunt. "I can't get over how big he is now," Anne said, as she made faces at the boy, who giggled in response.

"He just turned three," Stacy said. "He already recognizes some of the words in the books I read him."

"To hear Stacy tell it, the kid's some kind of genius," Sammy said.

"There's nothing wrong with being proud of him," Stacy said. "He *is* very smart."

"He's a three-year-old, not Einstein."

The diners at the other end of the table ignored the bickering. Anne suspected they were used to it.

"Levi, open a bottle of champagne," Sam directed one of the guards by the door. "We should celebrate."

Levi did as asked, and passed full glasses of the bubbly. Sam stood at the head of the table and held his glass aloft. "To Elizabeth."

"To Elizabeth," the company echoed.

Anne cautiously sipped the bubbly. After so many months abstaining, she didn't want to end up lightheaded.

Lunch was grilled steak and roast potatoes, salad and asparagus and a lemon cake for dessert. "You're not eating much," her father observed after a while. "What's wrong?"

"It's all delicious," she said. "But I'm watching my weight." The truth was, her stomach was in knots. Why hadn't Jake answered his phone before? Had her father or brother sent someone after him as soon as she was out of the way? Or was he in some other kind of trouble? And was her father really going to let her walk away from here today, back to Jake and her life separate from the Giardino family?

She decided as soon as she could steal a moment alone, she'd call Patrick. She shouldn't have come here without telling him first, even though Jake had agreed to contact the Marshal when it was time to make the arrest. Patrick wouldn't have liked their plan and would have tried to stop her, but he had the manpower to protect her—and to protect Jake.

She turned to ask her father if he'd enjoyed skiing in Telluride, but his attention was focused on a car making its way up the drive to the house. "Who is that?" Anne asked.

"No one you need to be concerned about." Sam turned to the guard behind his chair. "Show our guest into my office," he said.

Anne pretended to focus on the food, but she watched the entrance to the dining room out of the corner of her eye. She could just see the front door from here. After a few moments, the door opened, and a white-haired man was ushered in. Was this the same man she'd seen at the gondola yesterday? The one Jake had identified as Senator Nordley? Had Jake been right that he was the one who'd engineered her father's escape? And was he here now to collect his payment?

PARTWAY DOWN the rock face, Jake realized he was probably clearly visible to anyone looking up from the back of the house. A bright blue jacket was not very good camouflage. He'd originally thought he could climb down quickly enough that being spotted wasn't much of a concern, but the rough terrain made the descent agonizingly slow. He spent most of his time clinging to the side of the mountain, plastered against the snow, freezing, his fingers aching as he clung to the barest projection of rock, praying he wouldn't slip and fall to his death. A lot of help he'd be to Anne then.

He'd missed her second check-in call. The one opportunity he'd had to pull out his phone, it had reported *No Service*. They'd discussed what he'd do if she failed to contact him, but had made no plans in the event that he didn't respond.

She was a smart woman, and not prone to hysterics. She'd be all right. He thought he would have heard gunfire, even at this height, if there'd been any trouble below. Of course, a small-caliber weapon with a silencer was another story.... He pushed the thought away and focused on inching farther down the slope. This next section of the climb was covered in deep snow, making it difficult to plan stable footing.

He stopped to rest, and to review his plans once he reached the house. He'd find cover, preferably with a view into the house, and try to locate Anne. If she was all right, he'd simply observe until she left safely, and he'd somehow make his way around to the road and back to the car. That was the most optimistic scenario, but not the most likely.

The most likely scenario was that there'd be trouble, probably when Anne tried to leave. Though her brother had promised a happy reunion and safe passage, Jake couldn't believe Sam Giardino would give anyone who had betrayed him once—even his daughter—the opportunity to do so again. He might not kill Anne, but he'd make her his prisoner, and Jake would be the only one who could save her.

His determination renewed by this thought, he resumed his descent, pushing himself to move faster, to be bolder. He had no time to waste. If the Giardinos decided to move Anne to another location, he might lose her again, a chance he didn't want to take.

Clinging to a rock handhold, he lowered himself onto a narrow ledge and checked his progress. He'd made it almost halfway. The house, a sprawling assemblage of glass and gray rock, looked much larger from this angle. If Jake moved faster, he could be to the wall directly behind the structure in another half hour or so. Encouraged, he positioned himself for his next step down.

The ledge gave way beneath him and he began to slide. He scrambled for a handhold in the rock, but found only loose dirt and ice. Snow filled his mouth and nose, and jagged rock tore at his clothes as he gained momentum, sliding and bouncing down the steep slope, unable to stop his fall.

Chapter Nineteen

The meal finally ended with coffee and brandy. Sammy had switched to scotch, despite the fact that it was only twelve-thirty. "I have to go the ladies' room," Anne said as they stood to leave the table. It was true, but she also hoped to use the opportunity to try Jake's phone again, and to call Patrick.

"Show her where it is, Stacy," Sam said.

Stacy, who was cleaning Carlo's hands and face, looked annoyed, but she handed the boy to Veronica and motioned for Anne to follow. Sammy grabbed his sister's arm as she passed. "Give me your phone," he said.

"No!" She tried to pull away from him.

"We can't have you sneaking off to call someone you shouldn't. Now, hand it over."

"Let go of me." She kicked him hard in the shin. He grunted and lashed out, catching her on the side of the face.

Levi moved to intervene, pulling Sammy away. Anne glared at him, and straightened her clothes. Her father came up behind her and put his hand on her shoulder. "You know I don't hold with manhandling women," he said. "But Elizabeth, I do need you to hand over your phone."

"If I don't check in with Jake, he'll send someone after me," she said.

"I'm sure we can deal with anyone who tries to get too close," Sam said. "You may have noticed when you drove in that this place is well-positioned for defense."

She'd counted six guards on the way in; there were probably twice that many out of sight, patrolling the grounds. They'd be well armed and well-trained, a private army sworn to defend her father from anyone he perceived as an enemy. Why had she and Jake ever assumed that Patrick had the forces at his disposal to take this place? Even if he could assemble a large enough force, he couldn't move in without risking the lives of innocent—or mostly innocent—women and children.

"Your phone." Sam held out his hand.

She surrendered the phone, then followed Stacy to the ladies' room. To her surprise, the other woman followed her inside. "Are you supposed to guard me?" Anne asked.

"I wanted to talk to you." Stacy glanced over her shoulder. "Alone."

"About what?"

"Why did you come back here?" Stacy asked, keeping her voice low.

"I wanted to see my father. And I wanted to find out who has been trying to kill me. Sammy says it isn't my father, and I think I believe him."

"I don't know anything about that, but you've stepped into the middle of a war zone. Your father and Sammy are at each other's throats all the time. I'm sure they're going to kill each other."

"Sammy's always had a temper, but he isn't stupid," Anne said.

"I used to think that, too, but now I'm not so sure. If I could get out of here with my son, I would. You were a fool to come back."

On that note, she turned and left, slamming the door behind her.

Anne used the bathroom, washed her hands and stepped out into the hall once more. Levi was waiting for her. "I'll take you back to your father, Miss Elizabeth," he said. He spoke in the tone of some staid family retainer. If she closed her eyes, she might imagine he was a butler or footman from a fine home at the turn of the last century.

But when she opened her eyes, his muscular build and the shoulder holster he wore in plain view would give away his true role. And to think she'd grown up accepting this as a perfectly normal way to live.

He led her, not to the great room where they'd been before lunch, but to a smaller side room that served as a study or library. Her father sat in a leather chair before a fireplace lit by a gas log, and motioned for her to sit across from him. "Is this your office?" she asked, remembering he'd instructed the guards to have his guest wait there.

"No."

"Don't you need to deal with your visitor?" she said. "I can wait."

"Don't worry about things that don't concern you."

How many times growing up had she heard those exact words? Strangers coming to the house, phone calls

in the middle of the night, the need to suddenly relocate for a few weeks or months—these were all deemed
matters that were none of her business. The women
in the family, including Elizabeth, were supposed to
keep quiet, obey and never ask too many questions.
She couldn't believe she'd accepted this role for so long,
though, as her father's clear favorite, she'd been allowed
more leeway than anyone else. Would he accept the
same degree of rebellion from her now?

"Elizabeth, tell me what you've been up to," he said.

She smoothed her hands across her thighs, and chose
her words carefully. "I've been fine," she said. "Staying busy." She wouldn't tell him she'd been living in a
small town and teaching school; he'd think such things
beneath her. All her life she'd heard how she wasn't like
"working people." He might even become angry if she
told him she'd become one of that despised lot.

"I've been thinking about what you said before," he
said. "About someone trying to kill you. I wonder if one
of my enemies sent this DiCello fellow after you as a
way of getting to me. Perhaps he wanted to frame me."

"Can you think of someone who would do that?"
she asked.

A ghost of a smile played about his lips. "I have
many enemies, but I can't think of one in particular
who would take that convoluted approach to revenge.
Or maybe DiCello knew about my outburst in court and
thought he could impress me and work his way back
into my good graces by doing me this 'favor.'"

"I thought you said he left to be closer to his mother
and sister."

Sam waved his hand in dismissal. "We had a bit of

a disagreement before he went. I thought his loyalties were too divided."

"Between you and who?" Who else would one of her father's men be loyal to?

"He and your brother had become good friends. Sammy thought he had the right to give orders to one of my people. I had to set him straight."

She winced inwardly. She was sure Sammy wouldn't have enjoyed that particular "lesson," which probably involved humiliating him in front of the men.

"Did you say this attack in your home wasn't the only one?" Sam prompted.

"After DiCello died there were two more attempts on my life," she said. "The fire in the cabin, and the car that tried to run us off the road."

"Two of my men disappeared last week, along with one of our cars," her father said. "I've been too busy with other matters to trace them, but I wonder if there's a connection." He leaned forward and patted her hand. "Let me check into it and see what I can find out."

Silence stretched between them while her father stared into the fire and Anne wondered how she was going to get away from here. "Would you please return my phone?" she asked.

"I'll get you a new one," he said. "One of ours." Meaning a phone on which he could monitor the calls, she knew.

"It's been wonderful seeing you again," she said, making her voice as gentle as possible.

"It's wonderful to have you back." He took her hand between both of his.

"I hope I'll see you again soon," she said. "But I can't stay."

"I'll send someone to your hotel for the rest of your things," he said. "Until then, I'm sure Stacy has clothes you can borrow if you need anything."

"Dad, I have to go." She pulled her hand from his and stood.

"You don't have to go anywhere," he father said. "Not now that you're back where you belong."

She backed toward the door, knowing there were guards there to stop her, but determined to try. She wouldn't quietly surrender to being made a prisoner. She would fight, and she wouldn't stop fighting.

A heavy hand on her shoulder stopped her. "You always thought you could get your way, didn't you?"

She smelled the scotch on her brother's breath before she turned to look at him. "Perfect Elizabeth," he sneered. "The child who could do no wrong. But you've done nothing but wrong lately. Starting with bringing a federal agent home and into your bed. You sold out your family for the sake of lust. Does that make you proud?"

"I won't have you talking to your sister that way," Sam said. "She's made some mistakes, but now she realizes she was wrong—"

"She doesn't realize anything. You didn't see them, Pop, I did. Her and that fed, two cozy lovebirds, plotting to hand you over to the authorities. As soon as she walks out of here, the agents will swoop in and lock you in handcuffs." He moved to stand between her and his father. "Don't you see, she's just here to betray you again. She's not your perfect little girl. She's a viper who wants to destroy you."

Sam stared at her. "Is that true?" he asked. "Did you really come here to betray me?"

"No! I wanted to see you. And to find out who was

trying to kill me and…" And to help Jake and Patrick arrest him again. To him, that was betrayal. To her, it was justice, but in this case they meant the same things.

"I already told you, I had nothing to do with those attempts on your life," he said. "You're my daughter, and you always will be."

"It would be better for all of us if you were dead," Sammy said. "I should have gone after Jake from the beginning. With him out of the way, you never would have survived the fire, or the drive to Telluride."

Anne stared at him, stunned and sick to her stomach. How could her brother, whom she'd loved, speak such hate-filled words? "Are you saying you were the one who was after me?" she asked.

"Samuel, what is the meaning of this?" her father demanded.

"I was doing it for you, Pop," Sammy said. "She didn't deserve to live after what she did to you. And with her finally out of the way, we could move on. You'd stop worrying about her and focus on me."

Her father's face was ashen. "You had no right," he said.

"I had every right. I'm the one who stayed home. The one who remained loyal. But it didn't mean anything to you." His voice shook, and his eyes were dilated, wild.

"Sammy, calm down," Anne said.

"No! I'm tired of waiting around for what is rightfully mine." He reached into his coat and pulled out a pistol.

"Sammy, no!" she screamed.

But it was too late. Sammy fired the pistol, the report deafening in the small room. Sam clutched at his chest, blood spurting between his fingers while Anne looked on, horrified.

While Sam was still falling, Sammy turned the gun on Anne. "You won't get away from me this time," he said.

She screamed, but the scream was drowned out by another gunshot. Sammy jerked back from the force of the blow, then sank to his knees. Anne stared at the window behind her father's chair, the glass shattered in a thousand pieces. Jake stepped through the opening, his gun fixed on Sammy. "Are you all right?" he asked Anne.

She nodded, too shocked to speak, then knelt beside her father just as her brother collapsed beside her.

THE DEEP SNOW had saved Jake's life, and delivered him to the house in record time. He'd ended up tobogganing down the slope on his belly and landing in an avalanche of thick powder at the base of the rock wall behind the house. He was banged up, with a rip in his pants and a gash in his leg that oozed a thin line of blood, but he was alive and whole—and apparently no one had noticed his spectacular descent.

He stood and brushed off as much snow as he could, then drew his gun, removed the safety and checked the load. All around him was quiet, and he saw no one. Keeping low and out of sight of the windows, he reached the back of the house, then crept around the side toward the sound of raised voices. Before he could identify the speakers, a gunshot shattered the silence.

Jake rushed forward, in time to see Sammy turn his gun on Anne. He fired, shattering the window and striking the younger man in the middle of the back. He didn't even remember stepping through the broken glass and moving to Anne's side. "Are you all right?" he asked.

She nodded, and knelt beside her father, but he was beyond help, his face forever frozen in an expression of surprise.

Jake turned to Sammy, who lay gasping on the rug, blood seeping from a hole in his chest. "We should call an ambulance," Anne said.

Jake thought it was too late for that, but who was he to say, considering how he himself had defied the odds? He looked for someone to make the call and found himself face-to-face with three men with guns, all of them pointed at him.

"Call 9-1-1," he ordered, ignoring the weapons.

No one moved. "Put those guns away and call for help!" Anne shouted.

The men looked at each other. "All right, Miss Elizabeth," one said, and the rest followed him out of the room.

Anne moved to her brother's side. He stared up at her, vacant-eyed. "Sammy, hang on," she pleaded, gripping his hand.

"I just…wanted him…to be proud…of me," Sammy gasped.

"He was," she said. "I know he was."

Sammy's eyes closed and Anne choked back a sob. Jake pulled her into his arms. "I'm sorry," he said. Not sorry he'd protected her, but sorry she had to go through this, to lose her family, no matter how bad they were.

Shouting and the sounds of running feet came from the front of the house. Jake stood, and pulled Anne to her feet behind him. "What's going on?" she asked.

"Jake! Anne!" a man bellowed.

"Patrick!" Anne called. "We're in here."

The U.S. marshal, dressed in black fatigues and carrying an assault rifle, appeared in the doorway of the room, flanked by two similarly clad officers. He took in the two men on the floor. "Sam Giardino and his son?" he asked.

"We need an ambulance," Anne said. "Sammy—"

Thompson was already kneeling beside the younger Giardino. "It's too late for an ambulance," he said. He moved to Anne. "Come with me. I've got a team ready to relocate you right away, before anyone here even realizes you're gone."

"I…" She looked around the room, confused. "Sammy's dead?"

Thompson nodded. "Come on," he said, one hand on her shoulder. "We have to go."

"Wait!" She wrenched away from him. "Senator Nordley. You've got to stop Senator Nordley."

"What about Nordley?" Thompson asked Jake.

Jake shook his head. "Is the senator here?" he asked Anne.

"He arrived while we were eating lunch and my father told one of his men to put him in his office to wait."

"And you're sure it was Greg Nordley?" Thompson asked.

"I think so. I only caught a glimpse, but he had white hair, and he looked like the man Jake pointed out to me in Telluride this morning."

"I have my men searching the house," Thompson said. "If he's here, we'll find him." He took Anne's arm again. "Now you need to come with me."

Anne stared at her fallen brother and father. "I can't just leave them," she said.

Thompson started to argue, but Jake stepped in. "Can't you see she's in shock? Don't ask her to make that kind of decision right now."

"Stay out of this," Patrick said. "We have to get all the women out of here. We don't know who else might move in to take over, and we need to take down their testimony before someone else gets to them. This is our chance to dismantle the Giardino operations while the family's in disarray."

"You can give her a little more time," Jake said.

"I tell you, we don't have time." Thompson turned her toward the door. "I promise she'll be safe."

Jake watched as the marshal led Anne away. Her head was bowed, and she moved blindly, letting Thompson guide her around the carnage in the room. Jake turned away, cursing under his breath. He shouldn't have let them take her—not like this.

"Sir? I need you to come with me."

He turned and faced another black-clad marshal. "We'll need you give a statement about what happened."

He looked over the man's shoulder, at Anne's retreating figure. "What will happen to her?" he asked.

"She'll be taken care of. You don't have to worry."

But of course, he would worry. And he'd start over, looking for her again. And this time, he wouldn't let her go.

ANNE SAT IN THE SMALL interrogation room, in an office whose location she couldn't have named, and stared into a foam cup of long-cold coffee. Patrick had taken her statement, then left her here to wait for the typed transcript, while he made the final arrangements for her to travel out of state. Tomorrow she'd start over—a new life, with a new name, a new occupation and a new past.

Before, she'd been grateful for the chance to make a fresh start. She'd longed to distance herself from her family, and from the pain of losing Jake. Now, all she felt was numb. Her father, a man she'd spent a lifetime both loving and hating, was gone. Her brother, who had been both ally and enemy, was dead, too.

And Jake. He was the one man who'd stood by her, and she'd realized his value too late. He'd saved her life, but more than that, he'd saved her from thinking she was only good enough to be her father's daughter, a pretty, spoiled socialite who turned her back on the suffering of others. Jake had shown her she had the courage to do the right thing—not once, but over and over again.

A knock on the door startled her out of her musings. "Come in," she called, and sat up straighter, trying not to look as exhausted as she felt.

Patrick leaned into the room. "There's someone out here who's asking to see you," he said.

"Who is it?" Patrick wouldn't let a reporter in to see her. But maybe Stacy wanted to speak with her. Or even Veronica...

Patrick held the door open wider and Jake came into the room. He stopped halfway to her. "I wasn't sure you'd want to see me," he said. "Now that you've had time to think about everything."

"Jake!" she cried, and ran to him.

He crushed her in his arms, and kissed the top of her head, over and over. "I'm sorry," he said. "I'm sorry about your brother and your father...and everything."

"Don't apologize for saving my life." She drew back,

just enough to look him in the eyes. "I'm glad I got to see you again. Thank you for coming."

"I couldn't let you go. I called Thompson and I made him tell me where you were."

"You must have been pretty persuasive. He thinks I'm still in danger from others in my father's business."

He cradled her face in his hand. "I told him I loved you and I didn't want to live without you."

Her breath caught, and tears stung her eyes. "I love you, too," she said. "And I don't want to live without you, either."

"Sounds like we're stuck." He kissed her, a sweet, gentle brushing of his lips against hers that said more to her heart than all a poet's words of love.

"I told Thompson I'd come with you into WitSec," he said.

"What about your career?" she asked. "Don't you want to get back into law enforcement?"

"You said yourself, I was never a typical agent." He smoothed his hands down her arms. "I'll find something to do. Don't worry about me."

"There's only one problem." Patrick moved into the room and shut the door behind him.

"What's that?" Anne asked.

"Jake's not in my budget. I can't enroll random people into Witness Security just because I feel like it."

"That's not a problem," Anne said.

"It isn't?" Jake sent her a questioning look.

"No." She took a deep breath. "I don't want to start over with a new life. I like the life I have. As Anne."

"Anne Gardener?" Jake asked.

She met his steady gaze. "Or Anne Westmoreland."

His grin erased all the weariness and pain of the past hours. "I like the sound of that," he said.

They kissed, and Anne marveled that so much sadness and happiness could be mixed up together.

Patrick cleared his throat, and reluctantly the lovers moved apart. "I can't guarantee your safety if you don't stay in the program," he said.

"I don't think I have anything to worry about now that my father and my brother are both gone," she said. "My father's business partners or his rivals will take over his operations, but there's no one left in the family to take over. And certainly no one who cares about me."

"We'll be offering protective custody to your sister-in-law and to your father's mistress," Patrick said. "You won't see them again."

"I understand." Jake would be her family now. The only family she needed.

"What about Senator Nordley?" Jake asked. "Was he at the house?"

Patrick shook his head. "No sign of him. He must have left before we arrived."

"I was in the bathroom for a few minutes right after lunch," Anne said. "My father might have sent him away then."

"We may ask you to confirm that he was at the house, but right now the investigation is ongoing." He put a hand on Anne's shoulder. "Are you sure you'll be all right?"

"I can look after her," Jake said.

Patrick studied them a long moment, then nodded. "All right. I'll take care of the paperwork. You're free to go."

She hurried to collect her coat, and to leave the office before Patrick changed his mind. Outside, it was snowing, soft flakes drifting down to dust her hair and the shoulders of her coat. Jake gathered her close. "It's going to be all right," he said.

"I know it will be." She kissed his cheek. In Jake's arms, she felt safe and warm, and more at home than she had ever been anywhere else.

* * * * *

Be sure to pick up Cindi Myers's
ROCKY MOUNTAIN RESCUE,
*coming out next month. Look for it wherever
Harlequin Intrigue books are sold!*

REQUEST YOUR FREE BOOKS!
2 FREE NOVELS PLUS 2 FREE GIFTS!

H HARLEQUIN®

INTRIGUE®

BREATHTAKING ROMANTIC SUSPENSE

YES! Please send me 2 FREE Harlequin Intrigue® novels and my 2 FREE gifts (gifts are worth about $10). After receiving them, if I don't wish to receive any more books, I can return the shipping statement marked "cancel." If I don't cancel, I will receive 6 brand-new novels every month and be billed just $4.74 per book in the U.S. or $5.24 per book in Canada. That's a savings of at least 14% off the cover price! It's quite a bargain! Shipping and handling is just 50¢ per book in the U.S. and 75¢ per book in Canada.* I understand that accepting the 2 free books and gifts places me under no obligation to buy anything. I can always return a shipment and cancel at any time. Even if I never buy another book, the two free books and gifts are mine to keep forever.

182/382 HDN F42N

Name	(PLEASE PRINT)
Address	Apt. #
City	State/Prov.	Zip/Postal Code

Signature (if under 18, a parent or guardian must sign)

Mail to the Harlequin® Reader Service:
IN U.S.A.: P.O. Box 1867, Buffalo, NY 14240-1867
IN CANADA: P.O. Box 609, Fort Erie, Ontario L2A 5X3

**Are you a subscriber to Harlequin Intrigue books
and want to receive the larger-print edition?
Call 1-800-873-8635 or visit www.ReaderService.com.**

* Terms and prices subject to change without notice. Prices do not include applicable taxes. Sales tax applicable in N.Y. Canadian residents will be charged applicable taxes. Offer not valid in Quebec. This offer is limited to one order per household. Not valid for current subscribers to Harlequin Intrigue books. All orders subject to credit approval. Credit or debit balances in a customer's account(s) may be offset by any other outstanding balance owed by or to the customer. Please allow 4 to 6 weeks for delivery. Offer available while quantities last.

Your Privacy—The Harlequin® Reader Service is committed to protecting your privacy. Our Privacy Policy is available online at www.ReaderService.com or upon request from the Harlequin Reader Service.

We make a portion of our mailing list available to reputable third parties that offer products we believe may interest you. If you prefer that we not exchange your name with third parties, or if you wish to clarify or modify your communication preferences, please visit us at www.ReaderService.com/consumerschoice or write to us at Harlequin Reader Service Preference Service, P.O. Box 9062, Buffalo, NY 14269. Include your complete name and address.

HI13R

THE SECRET OF CHEROKEE COVE
by Paula Graves

*Dana Massey's life is turned upside down, by both a family
secret and the offer of protection by the very sexy detective
Walter Nix.*

"What do you know about the Cumberlands?"

His back stiffened for a second at the sound of the name,
and he shot Dana a quick look.

"Why do you ask?" he said.

"My mother's maiden name was Tallie Cumberland. Ever
heard of her?"

Dread ran through him like ice in his blood, freezing him
as if he was still that little boy from Cherokee Cove who believed every tale his mama told him, especially the scary ones.

"You *have* heard of her."

"I've heard of the Cumberlands."

"Doyle says the most anyone would tell him is that the
Cumberlands are nothing but trouble."

"Does that sound anything like your mother?" he asked
carefully.

"No."

"Then I wouldn't worry about it."

Dana didn't say anything else until they reached the Bitter-
wood city limits. Even then, she merely said she'd told Doyle
she was going to stay at his house.

"Are you sure you feel safe there?"

"I'm armed, and I'm too wired to sleep."

"I could stick around."

"And protect the poor, defenseless girl?"

"Not what I said."

"I'm usually not this prickly. It's been an unsettling night."

"I'm serious about sticking around. Couldn't hurt to have an extra set of ears to listen out for danger."

"And it wouldn't hurt to have some extra firepower," she admitted. "But it's a lot to ask."

"You didn't ask. I offered."

"So you did." Her lips curved in a smile that softened her features, making her look far more approachable than she had for most of the drive.

Far more dangerous, too, he reminded himself.

"I do appreciate the offer to stay, but—"

"But you're a deputy U.S. marshal with a big gun?"

She patted her purse. "Glock 226."

"Nice." He bent a little closer to her, lowering his voice. "I have a sweet Colt 1991 .45 caliber with a rosewood stock, and if you quit trying to get rid of me, I might let you hold it."

A dangerous look glittered in her eyes. "You're trying to tempt me with an offer to handle your weapon?"

He nearly swallowed his tongue.

She smiled the smile of a woman who knew she'd scored a direct hit. "You can stay," she said almost regally. "We'll negotiate weapon-handling terms later."

Will Nix's protection be enough to keep Dana safe?
Find out in award-winning author Paula Graves's
THE SECRET OF CHEROKEE COVE,
on sale March 2014 wherever
Harlequin® Intrigue® books are sold!

INTRIGUE

HE PLEDGED TO PROTECT HIS NEIGHBOR, IN *NEW YORK TIMES* BESTSELLING AUTHOR CYNTHIA EDEN'S SHADOW AGENTS: GUTS AND GLORY MINISERIES.

When Gabrielle Harper's gutsy investigative reporting attracted a serial killer, her new neighbor began keeping watch. But Cooper Marshall was more than his chiseled frame suggested. He was an Elite Operations Division specialist who thrived on adrenaline and whose every instinct was geared to protect—even if it meant breaking cover. Gabrielle wasn't the sort to hole up in her Washington, D.C., walk-up, waiting to be the next victim. So when the time came, he'd throw her on the back of his motorcycle and ride with a vengeance to save her life. Until then, he'd watch and wait....

THE GIRL NEXT DOOR

BY CYNTHIA EDEN

Available March 2014, only from Harlequin® Intrigue®.

INTRIGUE®

A SMALL-TOWN INNKEEPER'S LIFE IS TRANSFORMED BY A SEXY ARMY RANGER IN *USA TODAY* BESTSELLING AUTHOR CASSIE MILES'S SNOWED IN.

Rescuing a beautiful woman from four armed men wasn't how Blake Randall had planned to spend his army leave. But as chief security detail at his best friend's wedding, the ranger's mission is just beginning. A blizzard has cut off Sarah Bentley's Colorado B and B from the outside world, trapping them with a killer. Blake will keep the spirited innkeeper safe—whether she wants his protection or not.

Snowed in with the rugged stranger who already saved her life once, Sarah has no choice but to trust Blake. As passion ignites, she realizes he's so much more than a strong shoulder to lean on. With the danger escalating, it's time to listen to what her heart's telling her: with Blake by her side, they can survive anything....

SNOWED IN

BY CASSIE MILES

Available March 2014, only from Harlequin® Intrigue®.

HI69748